# UNSEX ME HERE

# Also By Avtar Simrit

TRUE TIME TRILOGY:
*A Dream of True Time*
*The End of Truth*

TRUE FICTION:
*True Fiction (Volume One)*
*True Fiction (Volume Two)*

POETRY:
*Shackled to Creation*
*Break Every Chain*

THE COMPLETE LYRICS
OF AVTAR SIMRIT:
*Nilotic Years*
*The MC Pan Era*

THE CKASPIAN CHRONICLES:
*Unsex Me Here*

# UNSEX ME HERE

AVTAR SIMRIT

To David James Isaac Woodley White

# Contents

*"I'm not who I was, and I'm all the better for it.
So what if the island's working magic on me?
I need a little magic. I'm ready. Oh Lord,
I'm more than ready."*

- Clive Barker, *Galilee*

*The Kingdom of Heaven will come
when the two shall be one, outside
like the inside, the male with the
female, neither male nor female.*

# One

## Divine Androgyny

Calvin laid luxuriously on his couch—naked. The couch was red leather and stuck to his skin as he sweated. His hand was between his legs; but he wasn't working vigorously, he was stroking slowly, sensually. As he panted heavily, his blonde locks rolled down the sides of his face like a waterfall. When Calvin grasped his cock and stroked, he instead imagined his fingers sliding into an open vagina between his legs. Moaning and arching his back, he bit his lip as he squeezed his left breast and played with his nipple.

When the time of the climax arrived, semen squirted up his body out of the tip of his cock. However, in his mind's eye, he/she imagined a quick stream of liquid squirting from her pussy and soaking the couch leather. After several minutes of catching his breath, Calvin licked the gooey semen off his fingers. He let out a big sigh as he sat up on the couch. The contours of his body glistened with sweat as his dick now flopped flaccid between his legs.

The one bedroom apartment that Calvin rented was tiny. There was a small living room connected to the kitchen. Then there was just his bedroom and bathroom at the far end. After standing up, he walked gracefully to his bedroom, almost so smoothly it seemed he was gliding on air. Calvin's build was petite, and he had a small waist like a girl. He looked at himself in the full-length mirror he kept next to his bed. The mirror image showed a pretty young man who's facial features were feminine—high cheekbones and a smooth chin. But during these times of feeling girly, Calvin would tuck his dick back and gaze at himself in the mirror, willing there to become a *herself*.

"One day we can make you a woman," he said dramatically, pointing at himself in the mirror. "We have the technology!"

Calvin sighed and dropped his arm down to slap against his naked side. If a Blue Fairy magically flew into his window at that moment and asked him what his wish would be, he would say, "To make me a real girl! That my willpower would become magical and strong enough to transform my body whenever I wished it." However, no matter how many times he meditated and tried to *think* his body into becoming female, it never seemed to work.

Groaning with the realization that he had to get ready for work, Calvin let his penis pop back out from between his thighs where he had tucked it. He played with his testicles naturally as he pulled open the top drawer of his dresser. There was a red and yellow polo shirt he had to wear as a McDonald's employee. He took the shirt from the drawer along with a pair of black pants. Quickly he pulled them onto his slender body, put his hair back in a ponytail, and grabbed the visor off of the top of the dresser—that was part of the uniform as well.

Calvin's apartment building was basically right next to the McDonald's where he worked. This was convenient especially since he didn't have a vehicle. But he dreamed of leaving this town, Fallon, the town that he grew up in, for what he imagined were the brighter horizons of California. Sometimes he and his friends would make it into Reno for a night on the town, but Calvin longed for something more. The locals in the city would refer to Fallon as Fal-abama, and Calvin could understand why since *he* especially felt out of place in a town stuck in the past.

Rushing across the parking lot and through the front door of the McDonald's, he barely made it to clock in on time for his shift. He worked on assembly where he pulled the ingredients out of drawers and put the sandwiches together more like an architect than a chef. At least he had three friends who worked there with him, and their joking and laughing helped to pass the drudgery.

"What's up, blondie?" James said with a big smile as Calvin came into the back, tying his apron around his waist. "Greg and I were debating whether you were gonna blow off coming to work today."

Greg worked the grill and raised his chin in greeting as Calvin passed by. "Sup, bro?" Greg said.

"Well, I'm here," Calvin said with a smile.

"We figured that you'd have been up too late last night jacking off," James continued. "Then you'd have to call in sick this morning all, 'I'm so exhausted I can't come into work today, I drained all my man-juice life force last night spanking the monkey'." He did his best to put on a mocking voice impression of Calvin.

Calvin stuck out his tongue at his friend. "Fuck off," he shot back. "My life force *never* gets drained. My stamina is like *Dragon Ball Z* status."

"You guys are freaks," Casey said as she came over to the other side of the assembly table. She was Calvin's other friend. All four of them were best friends and had known each other since middle school.

"You calling *us* freaks," Greg shot back over his shoulder as he flipped the dog-meat on the grill. "Little Miss with her extensive butt-plug collection."

Casey went red in the face as James and Calvin burst out laughing. "I told you not to tell anyone about that," she whispered harshly. Casey wasn't a beauty by any stretch of the imagination. There was a fair amount of chub around her belly especially since she was a heavy beer drinker. Her skin was greasy and always had several zits on her face, and she kept her brown hair up in a scrunchie mostly because she was too lazy to brush it. She worked the drive-thru and wore one of those headsets over one ear. "Just fucking get those orders done," she huffed. "I've got people waiting at the drive-thru." Turning away from Calvin and James, she went back to her place at the drive-thru window.

"So, Calvin," Greg said as he threw another batch of fries in the deep fryer, "what was that you were saying before about you wanting to go traveling or some shit?"

Calvin turned to Greg who was working the grill and the fryer. He left James to do all the work assembling the burgers. Greg was maybe forty pounds overweight from eating fast food all his life. He wore a hairnet over his shortly cropped dark hair and his face sweated profusely from standing over a grill all day. Occasionally beads of sweat would drop from his chin and splash onto the filthy floor. If he could have, Greg would have been smoking a cigarette as he worked the grill, now and then ashing into the deep fryer.

"It would just be fun, y'know," Calvin answered, "to get out of Fallon for a while. Maybe see the coast of California. Maybe see Hollywood and then the Redwoods. I'd like to get a big van that I could maybe live in while I traveled. I mean, fuck, we've barely been out of this raggedy-ass town. And going to Reno doesn't count."

Greg shrugged. "Eh, I think you might find out that those other places aren't that much better than here anyway."

"Wow, you're a downer today, Greg," James said as he slid a Big Mac box toward Calvin. "Here, Calvin, put the fucking lettuce on this shit. At least pretend you're doing something." Calvin laughed and shook his head as he put the lettuce on the Big Mac, closed the box, and slid it down the line to be served to the customer. "But I'm with you, bro," James continued.

"Oh, yeah?" Calvin said, raising his eyebrows.

"Yeah," James replied. "We're the best-looking people in this place and—"

"Fuck you. Suck my asshole," Greg said over his shoulder.

"And," James continued, ignoring Greg, "we could have more than this. I wouldn't mind getting out of this dump too. We could be models—or actors."

Calvin smiled. James was a good-looking guy. Him and Calvin were the thinnest people and the best-looking in that whole fucking fast food joint—which wasn't really that difficult to be considering the type of people who worked in those places. James was short, but he was cute and had a slight build. He kept his blonde hair short, unlike Calvin, and used gel to keep it in a spiky style. Calvin had always been attracted to James and they even had a little thing when they were in high school, but it never went anywhere. James was too straight and Calvin was too queer for that to ever work out.

"Then come travel with me," Calvin said hopefully, smiling with a little blush on his cheeks at the prospect of living in such close proximity with—and probably sleeping next to—such a beautiful boy. "I know I've almost found the perfect conversion van to hippie around in. It would be like a dream." He brushed up against James's shoulder flirtatiously.

"Cut it out," James said, trying to suppress a smile. "I told you I'm not into that anymore."

Calvin ignored him. "We could be just like Thelma and Louise!" he exclaimed.

"And exactly just which one am *I* in that scenario?" James asked, raising his eyebrows.

"You'll always be Thelma to me, baby."

That night, Calvin was overcome with the determination to envision and create the new life he/she wished to live. After smoking some cannabis for inspiration, he practiced a short yoga set to get his body and blood moving in preparation for meditation. He breathed slowly and deeply as he sunk deeper into the meditation. Then he went to work visualizing and projecting what he wished to manifest. First he saw in his third eye an empty parking lot surrounded by tall trees. At first he thought they were Redwoods, but upon further scrutiny in his mind, he could see that they were an assortment of more common forest trees such as firs, pines, cottonwood, Sequoia, and others.

Quite suddenly a shape began to appear in one of the parking spaces. It was fuzzy at first, like a set piece on stage obscured by a fog machine, then it slowly solidified and morphed in his imagination. It began to wobble like a piece of Jell-O and turn green. It's shape and size was then like a small car. Then it began to stretch and grow as the color turned from green to red—or sort of burgundy. A word suddenly flashed through Calvin's meditation—*Quantum*. In that parking spot, clear as day, was now a decently sized conversion van; something that Calvin would be comfortable in. He smiled to himself at the visualization and how seeing in the imagination was that much closer to manifestation. Then he saw himself appear standing next to the van—or was it *her*self? He—she—looked a bit different but largely the same. Maybe she had a little more flesh on the hips and ass, and he could see the small bumps of breasts under the tight shirt she was wearing. Her face looked slightly thinner and longer as well.

"Klarissa..." Calvin whispered. That was the name he had given his female form. "Goddess—or Blue Fairy," he continued loudly as if praying with his eyes closed, still focusing on the vision. "Whatever entity is listening, assist me in manifesting this vision into reality!" He suddenly opened his eyes into the darkness of his bedroom as if coming up for air from the bottom of a pool. "Make me a *real girl!*" He took a deep breath into his lungs and then blew all the air out forcefully in a cannon-breath as if to unleash his vision into the Unified Field to begin working its Magick.

Calvin let the vision fade from his mind and released it into the Spiralverse to become reality in whatever way the Chaos chose. After grabbing his laptop, Calvin flopped down on his bed and browsed the cars listed for sale on Craigslist until the effects of the THC took him over and he couldn't keep his eyes open any longer. The cannabis tinted his dreams purple. And in his slumbering psychedelic dreamscape, he might have caught the fleeting image of the beautiful, but alien, face of a blue-skinned woman with a smooth head and pointed ears.

# Two

## Avatars of Pan

Upon awakening, Calvin didn't notice the transformation which had taken place while he slept. However, he did notice right away that he had fallen asleep with his laptop open on the bed. He clicked the mouse touchpad lightly and the screen lit up immediately. The web-browser was still open to a Craigslist post. Calvin squinted his eyes and rubbed the sleep out of them so he could read what it said. As he scanned the picture and text, he couldn't remember seeing it the night before. The photo in the post was of a red Dodge Ram conversion van—the spitting image of the van he had seen in his visualization. Calvin's mouth hung open in astonishment. *Am I still dreaming?* he wondered.

The van was marked at three thousand dollars. *Three grand,* Calvin thought to himself. *Like three wishes; a grand for every wish.* The blurb said that the vehicle ran perfectly and was in good shape for a high-mileage van. At the bottom it read: *Direct all inquiries to Avtar Simrit*—and there was a cell phone number. Calvin grabbed his iPhone off of the bedside table and dialed the number on the Craigslist post. A sleepy-sounding voice answered after a couple of rings.

"Yeah—" there was a yawn and then "—this is Avtar."

"Hi," Calvin began. He didn't know why he felt so nervous. "I'm calling about your post selling the red Dodge Ram van."

"You want to buy it?" Avtar said without any hesitation.

"Actually, yeah, I do," Calvin replied.

"I had a feeling you would call," Avtar said. Calvin almost thought he could hear a smug smile in his voice. "It's almost as if it was written in the stars. Huh, Klarissa?"

"Did I tell you my name?" he asked, his head spinning as if he had woken up in the surreality of a David Lynch film. "I don't think—"

"Yeah," Avtar continued, cutting him off. "You did earlier when I answered the phone." Calvin wasn't convinced, but Avtar just bulldozed right through that. "You got the money? You got cash?"

"I can, yeah," Calvin responded. "Cash—I can do cash. That'd be probably easiest actually." Avtar made a noise that indicated that was satisfactory. For a moment there was a lull in the conversation. Calvin broke the silence by saying, "I see your post says you're in California—Santa Ana? You don't mind driving all this way to Fallon, Nevada to drop off the van?"

"It's all good," Avtar replied like a good-natured hippie. "You're gonna need it anyway."

Before Calvin could comment on that, Avtar was asking for an address where they'd meet up and make the sale. Calvin gave him the address of the McDonald's. "I can be there by tonight," Avtar continued.

"Great... That's great," Calvin said.

"Sat Nam, Ji!" Avtar Simrit exclaimed, and hung up before Calvin even had a chance to say 'goodbye.' He closed his laptop and slid it to the end of the bed as he tossed his phone back on the bedside table.

"That guy was kind of weird," Calvin said out loud. Then he stopped, frowning, as if reacting to hearing his own voice for the first time. It sounded higher than he thought was normal. Suddenly his hands shot up to his chest and was at once cupping the contours of small teacup-sized breasts. "What the fuck?" he shrilled loudly and out of pitch. Pulling the collar of his t-shirt away from his skin, he looked down and shrieked at the sight of his own nubile breasts. He clapped his hands over his mouth to suppress the scream of shock which threatened to erupt from a throat that no longer had an Adams's apple.

*What was it that Avtar guy called me?* he thought to himself as he squeezed his eyes shut, almost trying to will himself to wake from this dream—if dream indeed it was. *Klarissa! He called me Klarissa! How could he have known?* Calvin—now *Klarissa*—was afraid to slide his hands down between his legs because...*she* knew what was going to be there. Or *not* there.

Swallowing hard, Klarissa ran her slender fingers down her thin neck, over her small breasts, down the curve of her waist, then over the boxers she was wearing to meet between her legs. It was *smooth*. It was such a new experience to not feel a cock and balls between her legs that she almost couldn't handle it. She kept asking herself: *Is this real? This can't be real.*

To get a better handle on what package she was working with now, she pulled up the band of her boxers and gazed at her new genitalia. Being a man just the night before, Klarissa almost felt like she had become a eunuch in her sleep. But she had more than just a smooth Barbie Doll crotch—she had a *cunt*. As she slid her hand down between her legs, shivers and gooseflesh traveled up and down her skin like it was a rollercoaster. An orgasmic tingle traveled through her pelvis as she stroked her finger over her clit for the first time. Then Klarissa gasped as her fingers found their way inside of herself. Her eyes were closed and she could feel the inside of her pussy getting wet.

"Uh...my god..." she moaned. And before she could really get into enjoying her new body, her eyes shot open and she freaked out. "Oh shit! Work!" she said, jumping out of bed as the anxiety began to take her. "They're gonna notice." She put her fingers up to the sides of her head, trying to rack her brain for a solution. "My fucking voice... My face is thinner and I'm more curvy. Will they believe I'm Calvin?"

Klarissa stripped off her t-shirt and boxers and stood naked in front of her full-length mirror. *Fuck, I'm hot!* Klarissa thought, trying not to turn herself on too much. Otherwise, she'd be stuck in the apartment all day pleasuring herself. After rubbing her clit for several minutes gazing at her own reflection, she had to force herself to stop and scramble to get ready for work. She found some gauze and a roll of bandages in the bathroom and used them to tape down her already-tiny boobs. "How the fuck do they do this all the time in the movies?" she asked herself. "*Boys Don't Cry* made it look so easy."

The irony was not lost on Klarissa that just the night before she was wishing to be a real girl, and now that she was one, had to pretend to be a boy again. "Just my fucking luck..." she mumbled, lacking proper gratitude for the magnitude of the miracle which had occurred to transform her. After putting on the rest of the McDonald's uniform, she put her hair back in a ponytail and put the visor on her head. Glancing into the mirror again, she thought she could almost perfectly pass for Calvin. Except for maybe the higher voice—she'd have to work on that; get some bass all up in that soprano.

Klarissa hustled to work, hastily clocking-in when she got there. Still catching her breath from the jog over, she took her normal spot behind the assembly station. Paranoia began to grip her. Greg was robotically flipping the burgers on the grill and James was now standing next to Klarissa giving her an inquisitive look. Klarissa darted her eyes over toward James and then quickly away. "What's up, bro?" she asked, trying to act as normal as she could. "Lots of orders and shit today?"

A smile slowly crept over James's face. "You're a strange one, Calvin," he said with a laugh. "You look..." he looked Klarissa up and down, "weird."

"Weird?" she squeaked. "What do you mean?"

"I don't know." James eyeballed her again. "*Sexier.* And why are you talking in a crazy deep voice? You sound like Batman."

"I am?" she said, trying to adjust her voice to more of a normal male range but not quite hitting it. Feeling her face flush, she put her hands up to her cheeks and felt sweat beading around her hairline. "Sexy? Aw, do you really think so, babe?" she said, pretending to be pretending to be embarrassed.

James laughed and shoved Klarissa in the shoulder. "Nah, bro. I was just fucking around with you—see if your head would get big."

The rest of the day felt like a normal work day, and Klarissa felt like her co-workers weren't picking up on the fact that she wasn't Calvin anymore—or at least if they were, they didn't let on. It did seem odd to her though, of course, that her friends seemed a bit quieter than usual and were a little stand-offish when around her. At one point during her shift, she even noticed James had snuck off and he was in the back with Greg and Casey; they were whispering amongst themselves and occasionally stealing glances in Klarissa's direction.

At the end of her shift, Klarissa couldn't get out of that McDonald's fast enough. It was getting dark and when she was walking through the parking lot of her apartment building, she noticed a red conversion van parked in the middle. There was a short, slim person leaning up against the van like he owned it. He wore a white turban and white flowing clothes as if he was about to go attend service at a Sikh Temple. *This must be Avtar Simrit,* she thought, getting excited at the prospect of her new vehicle. She noticed a smaller car—looked like a Subaru—parked next to the van, and there was another guy wearing a turban who was snoozing in the driver's seat.

Avtar pointed at Klarissa as she approached. "Klarissa, right?" he said. She nodded. His face lit up and he opened his arms like he was expecting a hug. "Sat Nam!" Avtar exclaimed enthusiastically. Klarissa haltingly went in for a hug with this stranger. His embrace was surprisingly warm and comforting, like he was connecting her heart to the peace of the Divine. "You are even more lovely in person," he continued, kissing her on the cheek and then disengaging from their embrace.

"Thank you," Klarissa said shyly. "How did you kn—?"

"I know the *Shortbus* will be in capable and loving hands with you," he said, cutting her off.

"The *Shortbus*?"

"She is—*The Quantum Shortbus*," Avtar declared dramatically as he circled toward the back of the van. Klarissa followed silently. There was the word *Quantum* painted on one of the back doors in large flourishing letters.

"Is Avatar your real name?" Klarissa asked.

"Avtar, my dear. *Avtar*," he corrected. "However, you may refer to me as Mephistopheles." Avtar grinned widely, showing pearly-white teeth. Klarissa stared at him in stunned silence. "I'm just messing around," he laughed. "That's just a little joke I have going with the Most High—WaheGuru—"

"Bless you," Klarissa said quickly.

"Yes, exactly," he continued without a break, "but Avtar will do fine. It's my spiritual name."

"And what exactly are you an avatar *of?*" she asked inquisitively, not sure if she bought any of this weirdo's story. But then again, she had woken up this morning the opposite gender of what she was when she went to sleep last night.

"Pan, of course!" he responded definitively with excited reverence, like he deliciously reveled in the thought. "My dear, of Pan! Of Pan! Of Pan!" he chanted again.

"Like Peter Pan..." Klarissa whispered, almost to herself.

"He is one of us, I dare say," Avtar responded in a strange accent. Then his voice went back to normal and he asked, "I trust you have the fistful of mammon?"

"Ah, yes," she said too loudly, snapping out of her Peter Pan trance. "Let me run upstairs real quick and I'll get it."

Avtar nodded his approval and Klarissa quickly scuttled up to her apartment. She had a portable safe that she kept her stashes of cash inside. It was shoved in one of the top shelves of her bookcase in the bedroom. After punching in the combination on the keypad, the safe popped open to show stacks of hundred dollar bills—more money than you would expect for someone working at McDonald's. She grabbed three grand and rushed back down to pay for *The Quantum Shortbus*—the van that to her imagination looked like a psychonaut starship.

When she got back down to the parking lot, Avtar was smoking the remnant of a pungent blunt. He handed it to her when she approached. She raised her hand and said, "Thanks, but I'm good right now."

"Oh, come on," Avtar prodded, reaching the smoking roach closer to her. "Toke up to celebrate your new acquisition."

Klarissa broke down and took the remains of the blunt as she handed him the cash. "It's all there, you can count it," she said as she took a deep hit off the blunt.

"I trust you," he assured her as he slipped the money into his pocket uncounted.

Klarissa coughed hard from the harsh hit of the weed. "Holy shit," she said, handing the blunt back. "What kind of weed is *that*?"

Avtar chuckled like a trickster god who just played a delicious prank on an unsuspecting mortal. "I call it *Cosmic Shipwreck*." He said it with pride. "It's like, y'know, *Trainwreck* in space..."

"Oh, I get it," Klarissa returned, her legs starting to feel wobbly and her mind swam from the effects of the THC. "You gonna..." she trailed off.

"Oh yeah, I got all the paperwork for you and title transfer and shit," Avtar said hastily, taking a few quick hits off the minuscule roach before tossing it onto the concrete of the parking lot. He filled out all the paperwork for Klarissa, and used the info on her 'Calvin' driver's license without even making a comment about it.

"Thanks, I really appreciate this," Klarissa said as she folded up the paperwork and took the key from Avtar's hand.

He stared deeply into her eyes and spoke, saying, "May we retrace each other's paths and meet again in outer space."

Klarissa didn't know what to say to that and didn't have a chance to because Avtar wrapped her in another hug. "You are gorgeous. You are God. And *We* are Pan," he whispered and let go of Klarissa. His friend was now waking up and moving around the driver's seat of the Subaru. Avtar gave a little bow and as he walked away said, "Sat Nam and Wahe-Guru!"

Klarissa watched as the strange turbaned person jumped into the passenger's seat of the Subaru and then they sped away into the Nevada night. She shook her head, half expecting to wake up and this all have been a dream. When she realized that the key to her new van and the paperwork were not going to dissolve in her hands, Klarissa gave a long sigh and went back up to her apartment for some much needed rest. The adrenaline of the day was wearing off and the tiredness made the dreamlike even more dreamlike. Oh—and she was high as fuck! *What kind of weed would a cosmic turban guy have?* she wondered. Could it send her into another dimension?

That was her thought as she drifted off to sleep. Maybe that had something to do with her freaky-ass dreams. In this dream she was traveling as particles on a stream of light—of rainbow light that curved into a spiral. And as her dream-consciousness spiraled longer and longer, it stretched and compressed to create a hypersphere of space-time. The Spiralverse birthing in her imagination. At the end of the rainbow spiral was a gaping black hole. It was sucking everything into it—even the spiral, even consciousness.

Klarissa felt her particles dancing towards the threshold and couldn't escape the event horizon. Once into the Abyss, the Void, Klarissa felt as if she was being assembled and disassembled a million lifetimes ad infinitum throughout all of created experience. She was all things at once great and small—from a quantum spinning particle of dust to the most enlightened ethereal giant evolving into a planet or a galaxy. Then she was spit out, like being birthed into and by the blackness, the Chaos. He and She had been excreted into a fine jelly solidified into the beauty of an organism, reaching for divinity and orgasm.

The bed beneath her was soaked with sweat as she dreamed. And she scrunched her body into herself like a fetus. Her skin seemed to excrete a pink goo which didn't look unlike afterbirth. Out of her cosmic oneness she was jolted by a sharp knock at her apartment door. Klarissa's eyes shot open, still bloodshot from the *Cosmic Shipwreck*.

# Three

# Vehicle of the
# Psychonaut

"Who the fuck...?" Klarissa groaned, being rudely awoken from her weed trance. "What in the fuck time is it?" Reaching over, she flicked the little button on the side of her iPhone and the screen lit up, showing that it was a little after three in the morning. Rubbing her eyes as she slunk out of bed, Klarissa felt the floor with her feet for a pair of pants. Finding a pair of sweatpants bunched up on the carpet, she quickly pulled them over her slender legs.

Still half-asleep, Klarissa momentarily forgot about her transformation and mentally operated as if she were still Calvin. Looking through the peephole of her apartment door, she saw the faces of her three friends from McDonald's. They were all huddled on the porch speaking to each other intensely in hushed whispers, then Casey shushed Greg and

James until they shut up. Klarissa opened the door, tired and irritated.

"What the fuck do you guys want?" Klarissa spit at them. "It's late as all ass-reaming fuck and we have work tomorrow—or did you forget?"

They ignored her as if she hadn't spoken at all. "I think you should come with us, *Calvin*—or whoever the fuck you are," Casey said. There was madness and fire behind her eyes as if the Casey Calvin had known was now possessed by a demon of fury.

Klarissa's stomach sank as if someone had dropped a cinder block meant to drown a man. She suddenly remembered that she was no longer a man. Clinging to her baggy t-shirt, she tried to wrap it tighter around herself. "I'm Calvin. I'm Calvin!" she cried, voice cracking.

Suddenly Casey lunged forward and grabbed a handful of Klarissa's golden locks. She winced as Casey roughly jerked her head forward as if she was a rag doll being shaken in a dog's mouth. "You're going to tell us where Calvin is and what you did to him," Casey said as she dragged Klarissa down the stairs toward the parking lot, Greg and James trailing behind. "What are you, some kind of identity thief?" she said with disgust.

"I'm Calvin, I swear," Klarissa pleaded. "You guys are fucking crazy. I didn't *do* anything!"

All three ignored her attempts for reason. They herded Klarissa over to Casey's truck and rudely pushed her into the backseat. Greg got in beside her to make sure she didn't try to run; he outweighed her by almost three times. Casey hopped in to drive and James sat beside her. He turned around in his seat to look at Klarissa as Casey sped away into the night. "I *know* Calvin," James said, looking her all up and down, "and you are *not* Calvin."

"I am—" she started but was cut off by James.

"*Calvin* had a dick and balls—"

"Why? You seen 'em?" Casey snorted.

"Maybe..." James replied, getting red in the face. "Shut up, you slut. You're not one to judge me." Casey shrugged her shoulders and James turned back to look at Greg. "Check if she's got a cock and balls." He raised his eyebrows and indicated with his head.

Greg licked his lips and moved his fat sausage fingers over the inside of Klarissa's thigh. She closed her eyes and cringed as she felt his chubby hand grope between her legs. It was smooth, definitely no male genitals. "That is definitely a woman," Greg confirmed, letting his hand linger too long and then mercifully stopped molesting her.

"*See*! I fucking told you—I fucking *told* you guys!" James exclaimed to his friends, gloating over his accuracy of assessment. "Calvin ain't no woman," he continued. "I've fondled his balls. I've had his cock in my mouth. He most definitely had that equipment. So who the fuck *are* you?"

Klarissa didn't know what to say. She cowered in the backseat of the pickup truck, trying to will herself to become smaller. After a long drawn-out silence, Klarissa managed to squeak out, "What are you going to do with me?" She was suddenly afraid of her friends, as if they were foreign entities—aliens that had snatched their bodies, and the only thing left that was familiar was their skins.

"Well, that depends on you, sweet-cheeks," James retorted in a mocking tone.

"I don't know what to tell you," Klarissa said, sputtering and exasperated. "I'm Calvin... I'm Calvin... I'm Cal..." She couldn't even finish the word because she had begun to cry, shaking from the sobs. It was as if she was mourning her own death.

"Quit lying!" Casey suddenly screeched. "Did you kill him? You fucking killed him, didn't you?" She looked into her rearview mirror to see Klarissa and her eyes threw flaming daggers. Klarissa was stunned upon hearing this version of Casey which she'd never seen. It almost sounded like she actually cared what had happened to Calvin. Almost in a way a lover might be concerned about their partner. *Did she like me? Did she want me?* Klarissa asked herself. *I never figured Casey liked me or cared about me like that.*

Casey brought the truck to a stop, parked it, but left the headlights shining. "Maybe standing over your own grave will help you remember what you did to Calvin," she said in almost a whisper.

Klarissa wanted desperately to say something, but what kind of explanation could she give? There wasn't a way that she could prove her story of still being Calvin. But neither could they prove Klarissa killed Calvin to steal his identity. They were just blinded by some rage that Klarissa didn't quite understand. In an instant her door was swiftly pulled open and Greg kicked her out of the truck and onto the dusty desert ground. Casey stood over her, laughing. Leaning down, James grabbed the collar of Klarissa's t-shirt and dragged her into the light of the pickup truck's high beams. "We gotta know for sure that this imposter is not Calvin," Casey yelled over the hum of the engine. "Maybe she grew a penis in the last fifteen minutes. James! Why don't you check again."

Klarissa was on her knees and without warning, James delivered a swift kick directly to her face. As his boot collided with her jaw, her head snapped back and she collapsed onto the ground. She groaned half-consciously as James tugged on her sweatpants, eventually pulling them all the way off and kicking them aside. Then he pulled her shirt off and cupped her breasts in his hands, pinching her little nipples. He grinded the crotch of his pants against her bare ass. Greg and Casey stood and watched as blood seeped from Klarissa's mouth and hairline.

"Why don't you just fuck it, James," Casey taunted. "Whatever *it* is."

James's head snapped up and he looked at Casey. "You want me to fuck this *thing*?"

Casey smirked wickedly and nodded her head. As he opened his pants, James was already semi-hard, and it didn't take long for his cock to get rock-hard pressed against Klarissa's supple ass. She moaned as he penetrated her deeply.

"Does her pussy feel like rubber?" Casey asked; she had her hand down the front of her pants and was teasing her clitoris as she watched the live rape in front of her. Greg watched the show, but he wasn't touching himself.

"No... Uh, god," James moaned. "Feels like an all-natural wet cunt to me."

"Don't cum just yet," Casey said as she walked to the side of her truck and reached into the bed. She pulled out a long blade and removed it from its sheath.

"W-what are you gonna do?" Klarissa slurred, not quite awake and not quite unconscious.

As if in answer, Casey swung around and kneeled next to Klarissa's head as it bobbed up and down with each thrust of James's hips. She got ahold of Klarissa's head by her hair and then put the blade lightly against her throat. "Now answer me again," Casey said slowly, almost hypnotically, "did you kill Calvin?"

"Yes, I fucking killed him," she finally answered, spitting blood and feeling the throb of the hard cock up in her. "I assimilated him," she continued manically, spraying blood from her lips. "I distilled him into vaginal goo and absorbed him. Then I shoved his remains in my pussy while reciting a litany to Pan. I became the clone of his copy and negative image. Unsex me here, and Calvin was no more!" Her hiss echoed deep into the chill of the desert night.

"That's what I thought you'd say," Casey commented with a deep scowl.

"Oh, fuck, I'm gonna cum soon," James groaned as he fucked Klarissa's hole raw and with increasing speed.

"Cum!" Casey screamed. "Give her your juice!"

James shrieked out a moan and ejaculated at the exact moment that Casey sliced across Klarissa's throat. Her blonde hair was soaked red as blood squirted from the gash. Choking and gurgling, her face smacked into the ground, a pool of blood spreading out around her head. Klarissa's tongue flopped around her mouth as she drowned in her own gush of blood. *He's still inside me,* she remembered thinking. *I can still feel his hard cock inside me.* He only pulled out once her heart ceased to beat, a trail of semen dripping from his tip and into her dead snatch.

Casey wiped the bloody knife on her pants and then returned it to its sheath. After tossing the knife back in the bed of the pickup truck, she pulled out two shovels from back there. "Here, and I hope you're not superstitious," she said as she handed the shovels to Greg and James. "So you best get digging quick, or each of us just might end up digging two graves."

# Four

## Vengeance In Mind

Only moonlight shined over the desert spot where they had killed Klarissa. Her body laid in a shallow grave as the shadowy translucent image of a figure appeared in the darkness of the night. It was the blue-skinned woman. Her head was smooth and her ears were tall and pointed. She wore a long flowing blue dress. After leaning down, she whispered something into the dirt and then disappeared.

In a wind-whipped moment, a hand shot up out of the earth. It was Klarissa's arm, white with the desert's dirt. Before long she had squirmed her way out like a worm. She was weeping, naked and covered in blood, but the gash across her neck was gone—gone like Calvin's genitals. Without fully realizing what was happening, Klarissa stumbled forward, hoping that she was walking toward Fallon.

She was so delirious from the trauma of dying and then coming back to life, that she blacked-out and it was as if she was sleepwalking all the way back to her apartment building. Coming back to awareness, Klarissa started remembering what had taken place. Rage suddenly gripped her as she became painfully aware of the chill that went all the way to the bone. She needed to get inside and get some clothes. The door was so close. Her teeth started to chatter as she got to her apartment. It was still unlocked and she greeted the warmth within as a welcome comfort.

After Klarissa finally got some clothes on, her brain began to twirl like a hamster wheel. *How could they do this to me? These are my friends? Who the fuck are they? I've never seen them act like that.* It made Klarissa wonder how well can you really know a person. Not at all, she guessed. No one really knew her either. Who was she? This Klarissa? Or was Calvin still hiding inside?

But she didn't care about that now. Her mind was hellbent on revenge. They murdered her so their lives were forfeit. That was only fair. So she grabbed a folding knife out of her dresser drawer and vowed that she would slit their throats like they had slit hers. Grabbing the keys for her new van, she thought, *might as well drive.*

James lived in a secluded little neighborhood. It was the house that he had grown up in and he still lived there with his mom. There were many times, Klarissa remembered, when they were kids and would sneak in and out of his house without his mom knowing. So she knew exactly how to get into James's bedroom.

Klarissa parked down the block so her headlights wouldn't be noticed by James or his mom. Then she snuck out silently, like a transexual ninja, to bring the wrath of the night. With light footfalls, she circled around to the back-yard to creep up to James's window. It was never locked. Tonight was no exception. She slid it open and then vaulted herself into the room like she had done a hundred times before.

James snored quietly on his bed—as if he hadn't just committed rape and murder. Klarissa glanced around, remembering fondly times she spent in here with him. But that time was over. That was a different time, a different life, when she was a different person. Tears burned as well as anger—and a deep visceral despair that this was how their friendship would end. Klarissa raised the knife above James's sleeping form.

"Stop!" a voice said sharply.

Klarissa froze, not knowing where the voice had come from. Quickly she glanced toward James's desk and computer, and then his TV. She didn't see anything. So, licking her lips, she readied her knife again to deal the death blow. Suddenly, before she could act, the image of a form began to appear in front of her. It was a woman leaning over James's sleeping body, as if to protect him, and was looking up toward Klarissa. This woman had long pointed ears, a smooth bald head, and blue skin. *It's the Blue Fairy!* Klarissa thought. She stood there, with her mouth hanging open, staring at the holographic form of the blue woman.

"You don't want to do this," the blue woman pleaded. "It will chase you—it will follow you forever."

She was right, Klarissa thought. Hesitating, her hand grasping the knife dropped slightly. She wondered if James would wake up. He groaned and shifted around in his sleep, but then went back to lightly snoring. "What am I doing?" Klarissa whispered to herself, putting the knife away.

"You could just get out of here," the blue woman continued. "Go start a new life. Maybe reach for the stars. You make the rules in your own spaceship." She smiled and then put her hands together as if she was praying, bowed slightly, and then disappeared. Klarissa shook her head vigorously, as if trying to see if she could knock the crazy loose from her brain.

She got the hell out of there. After sliding the window closed, she ran back to her van, eager to be rid of this town and these people. Good thing she didn't have all that much stuff at her small apartment. She made quick work of packing her worldly possessions into *The Quantum Shortbus*. Anything that was too big or impractical, she left behind. Who cared? Technically she was dead—or *he* was dead, rather. Or both, maybe. Regardless, she was still standing and in a relatively stable state in spite of an overnight magical sex-change and a murder—her own for that matter.

With the aid of a large pot of coffee, in a few short hours, *The Quantum Shortbus* was ready to go. Klarissa kissed her old apartment, old life, and old McDonald's goodbye, and left them behind in her cosmic dust. It was time for the sunny skies and infinite horizons of California. Wired on caffeine, she drove long and deep into the night.

On a long stretch of mountainous road, Klarissa reached for a joint that she had rolled and put in the ashtray before leaving Fallon. As she lit it and inhaled deeply, she thought about the ghostly blue woman. Who was she?

"You mean me?"

Klarissa bolted out of her weed-trance, seeing the semi-transparent blue lady appear next to her in the passenger's seat. "Are you real?" she asked, snubbing the joint out in the ashtray.

"Of course, I'm real," the blue woman laughed. But as Klarissa reached out to touch her, her fingers went into the blue light of her side. Inside, it felt like cold Jell-O, Klarissa thought.

"But you're like a ghost," Klarissa said, pulling her hand back.

"I'm not a ghost," the woman replied. "I'm only appearing to you in my plasma-body because my physical body is on a planet in the Pleiades far far away."

"Are you the Blue Fairy?" Klarissa asked in awe.

"I don't know what that is," she returned. "My name is Machandi—Pleiadian Goddess First Class."

"Ooo, First Class," Klarissa replied sarcastically. "Does that mean you grant wishes?"

"Something like that," Machandi said. "I was in deep meditation and I heard your prayer in the aether. I only came to assist with your situation."

"So it was you who made me into a girl?" Klarissa asked. This was what she really wanted to know.

"Klarissa," Machandi started, "you were already a girl—*and* a boy. You're a Zeromorph."

"A Zeromorph?"

"A Zeromorph," Machandi explained, "is an androgynous being able to hold the form of either gender—or both at the same time, theoretically. Yours was dormant, not quite hatched—or activated—yet. I helped it hatch."

"I feel like you're being purposely vague," Klarissa said, squinting her eyes at the dark road ahead of her. "I've been a man. I'm now experiencing being a woman. Am I now supposed to become a hermaphrodite? Huh, Machandi?"

The headlights of *The Quantum Shortbus* blinked for a second and Klarissa looked over into the passenger's seat. The blue ethereal form of Machandi had vanished. Picking up the rest of the joint from the ashtray, she sniffed it. "This must be some high-grade Sativa," she commented. "Seeing lights flicker, talking to blue people, thinking I don't have a dick..." Putting her hand between her legs, she had to remind herself that there was indeed a pussy there now. "Oh, yeah," Klarissa mumbled as the amnesia trance of the weed lifted and she remembered the events of the night. She cried as she crossed out of Nevada into California, purging the trauma out through her tear ducts.

# Five

Path of the Magician

Klarissa had driven all night until she reached Mount Shasta. After driving around a little, she found a cozy camp spot in the woods where she parked the *Shortbus*. Why had she picked Mount Shasta as her destination? She didn't quite know herself. There was a spiritual draw, coaxed by the influence of Machandi, that brought Klarissa to that spot. Had it all been a dream?

Calvin awoke in the marijuana fog. His arm had gone numb from sleeping on it weird. It would take some getting used to sleeping on a fold-down bed in the back of a van. As he yawned and stretched, Calvin touched his chest, which seemed flatter than it had been the day before. Then he noticed it—he had morning wood! *Morning wood? How could that be?* He frowned, picking up the light sheet he had draped over him. Sure enough, his erect dick poked out of the hole in his boxer shorts.

Had Klarissa manifesting all been a hallucination? Or could it have been a fever-cannabis dream brought on by adjusting to a new location and living situation? No use making questions of the unanswerable, Calvin thought after a while of waking up. He pulled on some sweat-pants and cracked open the side door of the van. Brisk Fall air swam into the van on a chilly breeze. It was colder than Calvin had expected, and he slipped on a hoodie and his sneakers. Even after stepping out into the cold morning air, Calvin's boner still raged, making a tent of the front of his pants. As the leaves crunched under his feet, he pulled his cock out and leaned over. With a sigh, he let loose the most welcome stream of urine. The relief washed over him as he drained the night's backup of piss.

It became flaccid as he shook it off. As he walked back toward the van, he noticed that the inside of his mouth felt like it had a slimy film coating it. Calvin pulled out his toothbrush and a bottle of water and hastily brushed the scum out of his mouth. After rinsing out, he spat onto the rugged ground of Mount Shasta. *Where can a man-lady get a coffee in this town?*

Calvin fired up *The Quantum Shortbus* and drove back down the dirt road toward the closest thing that counted for civilization. The town was small and quaint. Like an old town that had been forgotten and then revitalized by a couple of hippies who brought in trendy clothing shops and stores that sold crystals for insanely high prices. There weren't that many people out and about this early in the morning. Finally, in one little corner of the town, Calvin spotted just the place he was looking for. Above a little storefront inconspicuously hidden between the other businesses was a sign that read: *The Chai Shop*.

Calvin figured that sweat-pants were too sloppy to go inside wearing, so he dug out a pair of skinny jeans that were checkered purple and black. He brushed his golden hair and made it fall half in front of his ears and half behind, so his ears looked like they popped out on the sides of his head. Caffeine was calling to him from within the thought of a nice warm drink. Calvin hopped out of *The Quantum Shortbus* and gave her a little pat as he locked her doors. Then he walked into *The Chai Shop*.

The woman behind the front counter smiled at him warmly. She was a total hippie; with leggings that sported constellations, a casual dress that was purple and black, with a hemp belt wrapped around her waist. Her hair was dark, the color of chestnut, and so were her eyes. "Welcome to *The Chai Shop*," she said. "I'm Lilith."

"Good Morning, Lilith," Calvin said shyly, looking around at the cute little shop. There were New Age nicknacks: crystals, Tarot cards, incense, statues; as well as teas of all sorts. There was also a special 'book nook' room where there were rare books for sale and a little place to read. "Could I get a...uh...a chai?" Calvin said distractedly. "Dirty with three shots of espresso."

"I like a man who likes it dirty," Lilith flirted as she started getting the stuff ready to make the chai and prepping the machine. "I'm sorry," she continued, "I don't mean to misgender you. You do seem pretty androgynous. What are your pronouns?"

Calvin shrugged. "I don't know," he said weakly.

"Okay," Lilith replied and let the matter drop. She let the espresso drop from the machine into the cup. "I haven't seen you in here before. Did you just move into town?"

"Something like that," Calvin answered as he approached the counter.

Lilith suddenly got a mischievous look as she handed Calvin his drink. "Or did you come out magically from the caves of Mount Shasta? You do have sort of an Elven look."

Calvin smiled awkwardly at the strange compliments. "I came from around the Reno area. I needed a change of—oh, you know, just everything... How much do I owe you for the chai?"

"Oh," she said and looked at her cash register. "Six dollars and sixty-six cents."

"No shit?"

"No, yeah," Lilith replied. "That's about normal for that size."

"No, I mean—I just," Calvin started. "...The number...it's...nevermind." He gave Lilith a bill he fished out of his pocket and then put the change in the tip jar.

"Have you ever had your Tarot cards read?" Lilith asked, eyes wide. Calvin shook his head as he took a sip of his chai. "You have a very rare aura," she continued, reaching out her arm and running her hand through the space around Calvin's head and shoulder. "It's more neutral than anyone else I've ever encountered."

"Is that good?" he asked.

"It means you have very balanced masculine and feminine energies," she explained. "Yes, that's very good. First Tarot reading is free. How can you say no?" Lilith winked and pulled aside a curtain that was in the wall behind the counter.

"Okay, yeah," Calvin acquiesced and entered in through the curtain.

"Three shots of espresso?" Lilith said as she followed in after him. "You must want to get really wired."

Lilith took Calvin into her little temple that was lit by orange candle-light. They sat on the floor and Calvin noticed that one wall was full of books and that the rest of the room held statues of various deities as well as burning incense. She pulled out a deck of cards that was wrapped in crimson silk. As she shuffled, she told Calvin that the cards had been designed personally by Austin Osman Spare. He didn't know who that was, but he nodded and pretended that he was thoroughly impressed.

After Lilith shuffled them a bit, she handed the deck to Calvin who continued to shuffle them more. She closed her eyes and went into a little meditation. "While you're shuffling," she said, "think of your path, your predicament, or dream that you wish to fulfill."

Calvin shut his eyes while he was shuffling the Austin Osman Spare deck and channeled all of his energy into the cards so that it could divine the best symbols that he needed to see. Upon opening his eyes, he handed the deck back to Lilith. She laid out a spread in the shape of an eight-pointed star. While she flipped over the cards, Calvin noted all of them as they came; The Fool, The Devil, The Tower, The Lovers, The High Priestess, The Hierophant, The Three of Swords, and The Universe. Lilith put her hands up to her mouth.

"Oh my gods," she whispered.

"What? What is it?" Calvin asked anxiously. "Is that bad?"

With her finger, she traced the shape of the spread. "It's a path of the Magician," she said. When she saw Calvin's quizzical look, she continued. "It's *one* of the paths of the Magician. There are many paths of the Magician in the Tarot. And this one," she said dramatically, "is exceedingly rare. It's the path of the union of opposites—ultimately culminating in The Universe itself." She picked up the card to indicate it.

"Things here are already popping out at me," Calvin said, marveling over the artwork on the cards. "But what is your reading on this?"

"I see it mapping out the journey—the quest," Lilith continued, "of the Cosmic Magician. He—or she—or they start out their exploration a Fool, as one must, ignorant of the mechanics of the Spiralverse. The dog there, barking as the Fool gets close to the edge of the cliff, represents your instincts warning you of danger. That leads to the Devil card which is not necessarily evil in that sense. But the Magician must still be a Fool to fall for the Devil's tricks. However, it is a necessary evil. For you must still be a Fool to believe in a dream. So the Devil can also represent hope and lofty ambitions. The Fool pursues this dream foolishly with all his heart which causes mass upheaval—The Tower—which has to be the catalyst for the metamorphosis to occur. This change must be so catastrophic as to dismantle your whole life and force you to live in a new way. This expands your consciousness more and more to the point where you become your own lover. Your pursuit of knowledge and wisdom blossoms your feminine side. You fall in love with her—becoming The Lovers. This is all the mystical journey of the Magician's soul as it balances its own divine masculine and divine feminine. The Sacred Marriage within the Magician's Self gives birth to the wisdom of The High Priestess. It's interesting that she's there with The Hierophant. Which indicates to me that The Hierophant is using The High Priestess to teach you something about the wisdom of the feminine—of the Goddess. The Three of Swords shows that the lesson is harsh, but it is lessened by the love of The High Priestess within you. The lesson of The Three of Swords is achieving life through death. The number three denotes resurrection—specifically Christ's resurrection on the third day. Maybe you'll have to die, but you'll wake up to The Universe. That's here—that's this last card." Lilith pointed to The Universe card with its spirals, stars, and cosmic genitalia. "The Universe represents the All, or the Nothing, or the Cosmic Void. Or you could call it Pan—the eternal coming in and out of existence of All things."

"Beyond Duality," Calvin whispered as he took another sip of his chai.

Lilith smiled. "You catch on quick."

"That's a lot to unpack for one Tarot reading," Calvin re-marked, glancing down at the spread again. "I think I might go for a walk and meditate on all of this. It'll be good to see some more of the town, too. Thanks for the reading," he said, standing up to leave.

"It was my pleasure," Lilith said. "Come back and see me again soon," she added as she gathered up her Tarot cards. Calvin was already out of the temple and out of *The Chai Shop* shortly thereafter. Leaving his van parked by *The Chai Shop*, he strolled slowly down the sidewalk past the other shops and restaurants. *The Path of the Magician*, he thought. *I've never been into any of that stuff; Tarot cards, crystals, Kabbalah, magick wands.*

Calvin tried to put the shop owner and her strange card reading out of his head. Instead, he directed his attention to noticing the people that were now showing up around town. He noticed a pattern after a while. Half of the people seemed to be hippies in their twenties up through forties, who seemed friendly and waved and said 'hi' to Calvin as he walked by; the other half were old-timers who seemed like they'd been here in this town before the hippies showed up. These old-timers seemed to have permanent scowls on their faces—maybe they were seething with anger at having to share their town.

In such a strange mixture of vibes, Calvin wondered where in all this Chaos did he fit in—or *she* fit in?

# Six

# Moonflower

Calvin had gone to the local grocery store and stocked up on dry goods and canned food; enough to last him for at least three or four days, so he wouldn't have to go into town all the time. He liked the peacefulness of camping out in the woods. And between his meditations and walks through the trees, he found himself thinking of Lilith. She was immensely attractive. He thought of the dainty curve of her neck and the paleness of the skin of her collarbone. Her curves and her long legs. As these fantasies invaded his mind, the thoughts of the day that he had been Klarissa became all but forgotten. A different body with different memories.

It had been a couple days since Calvin had been back into town. His desire drove him back to *The Chai Shop* to see Lilith. She was there when he arrived. She was alone behind the counter and the rest of the shop was empty of people.

Calvin was greeted with a warm smile. "I was hoping I would see you again," she said.

"I'm back," Calvin replied.

"You're so different, so special," she continued, gushing over him. "I did some more divinations about you, and some enchantments to receive personal gnosis. You are powerful... You are powerful and you are mysterious." Calvin didn't say anything. "In my illumination, I discovered that you are an androgynous alien space being—or you will be one. That part was unclear."

"I don't know about alien," Calvin replied more confidently. "But I can show you my spaceship."

Lilith swooned and flushed. "Don't tease me with promises you can't keep," she flirted.

"Can I get a chai? Same as before?" Calvin asked, switching gears.

"Yeah," she said, pulling a cup from the stack. "Go check out the books." She indicated the 'book nook' room. "There's a lot of great and strange stuff in there. Go—I'll bring your tea."

"Thanks," Calvin returned and then walked over into the room with all the rare and occult books. He browsed through the shelves of books, running his finger along their spines. When he came to a book with a blue cover, he stopped. After pulling it from its home on the shelf, he read the title: *At the Sign of the Square and Compasses*. There was a little chair with a table next to it where Calvin went to sit down and flip through the book. As he flipped through the contents and the pages of the book, Calvin saw that it was all about the Craft of Freemasonry—a subject that he knew little about.

A few minutes later Lilith came in and sat his drink down on the little table. He picked it up and drank it as he put the book down. Lilith scanned the shelves for a specific book and Calvin eyed her as she did. After finding the right one, she plucked it from the shelf and came back over to Calvin. She plopped right down on his lap and showed him the book. It was a large paperback with the title: *The Art of Sexual Magic.*

"Have you ever done any Sex Magick?" Lilith asked with large eyes as she stroked the side of his face.

"I can't say that I have," Calvin answered.

"Sometimes you can manifest the most unlikely of things." She pulled the book from his hands and set it on top of the Freemason hardcover. Then she leaned in and kissed Calvin on the lips. "You're so cute," she continued. "I want you to make love to me like OSHO. He was never born and he never died. The Master came down from space and then returned to space."

Calvin didn't know what to say. Lilith put her finger up to her lips and smiled wickedly. "Now?" Calvin asked.

"There's no time like Now," she said with a giggle. Hopping up from his lap, she grabbed his hand. "Come," she said as she led him out of the book nook. Quickly she locked the front door and spun the sign to say *Closed.* Back past the curtain that was behind the front counter, next to Lilith's little temple was a staircase leading up to the second floor where she lived. The upstairs was like a small apartment. It was basically a bedroom with a small kitchen attached and a small bathroom with a shower. The bed was big and took up half of the room. The floor was carpeted in a drab yellow shag. And there were books—lots of books—stacked up along the perimeter of the room. Calvin also noticed two distinctly different laptops.

Lilith jumped on the bed and patted the spot next to her, inviting him to join her. "Come on," she said. "I don't bite unless you want me to."

"That can be fun," Calvin remarked.

Lilith took that as a hint and leaned forward, putting her lips and teeth around the side of his neck. He cried out as she bit down hard. He winced at the pain as she pulled her head back, a dab of blood in the corner of her mouth. "What's Magick without a little blood?" she said, batting her eyelids.

"That fucking hurt," he responded, touching his neck.

"It was supposed to."

She laughed as he pounced on her, kissing her neck, face, and lips. Pretty soon Lilith was pulling at Calvin's clothes. She pulled his shirt up over his head, revealing his skinny pale twink torso. They continued to make out as they got each other naked. Calvin was hard and sweaty as Lilith licked down his body and then put his cock in her mouth. She massaged it with her tongue as he moaned. He imagined that he was in Klarissa's body and that it was a clit that Lilith was sucking on.

She pulled his cock out of her mouth and looked up into his eyes. "I want you inside me," she whispered. "I want your alien to probe me." Laying down on her back, Calvin got on top of her. She was so wet that it didn't take much for him to slide right in. Her mouth hung slack as she tilted her head back in ecstasy. He penetrated her in slow, steady strokes that built the orgasm up slowly, like a Tantric Master. "We're making the Magick," Lilith whispered in his ear. "Can you feel it?"

Calvin could feel an energy awakening at the base of his spine. It tingled like a surge of electricity. He could feel it uncoiling like a snake and then start moving up his back. "The energy is moving," he commented.

"It's wonderful," Lilith luxuriated. She flipped Calvin over and got on top, riding his androgynous cock. "It's moving through the Chakras," she continued. "Once the Kundalini hits the pineal gland, we will orgasm in our sixth Chakra and in our genitals. That's when you hold the image in your imagination of what you want to manifest. This is Sex Magick," she finished breathily. They were getting close to climax.

Calvin closed his eyes as he felt that he was about to explode with cum. Then he visualized it—Klarissa. He saw himself as Klarissa again in his Third Eye. Suddenly, in his imagination, the desire became represented in words, then the words became deformed letters which arranged themselves into a sigil that represented that desire. The sigil shone with a beam of light in his mind as the orgasm exploded in his head and out of his dick. They both yelled out with the euphoric pleasure of the whole mystical experience. Then Calvin let the sigil and the desire dissolve into the Spiralverse.

They opened their eyes, panting. Calvin looked up at Lilith and put his hand over her heart Chakra. She smiled warmly and put her own hand over his. "That is the best way to make Magick," she said.

Calvin's head spun and he thought he saw swirling patterns of light all around them. Sitting up, he kissed Lilith on the lips. Then he felt it—some strange tingling in his genitals. It felt like they were *changing*. Calvin suddenly pulled out of her and she fell onto the bed with surprise. "There's some stuff I gotta do for the rest of the day," he said hastily.

"Okay, Tantric Master," she replied sorrowfully. "Come back soon and we'll do some more Sex Magick."

After kissing Lilith with his tongue for a little longer than he should have, he scrambled to get his clothes on. He scampered out of *The Chai Shop* so fast that all Lilith could do was sigh and touch her breast.

Calvin barely got back to his campsite before his body started to change. The sensations in his body were so strange he had to jump onto his fold-down bed and stretch out. He felt his chest growing into breasts. It was the strangest feeling to have flesh added onto his body in seconds. Then his genitals shrank. That was the part that freaked him out. He pulled his pants down and watched as his cock and balls disappeared out of existence. It felt to him like the whole organ was being sucked into a vacuum cleaner. Then the flesh split, creating the vulva. He felt the clitoris bloom from between the pussy lips. The weirdest sensation, that gave her chills, was just then when the inside of her opened up.

"Oh my god," Klarissa said, catching her breath. She felt high from the aftermath of the Zeromorphic transformation. "It's fucking real. I did it." Sitting up on the van bed, she looked around the back of the vehicle. "Blue Fairy? Are you here?"

Klarissa felt a disembodied presence for a few moments before the semi-transparent blue form of Machandi appeared sitting cross-legged on the floor of the van. "My name is Machandi. And I am here. This is for you, Klarissa. Are you happy?"

"Well...yeah," she replied. "I Zeromorphed during the day—while I was awake!"

"Zeromorphosis," the blue alien goddess said. "You casted a spell for that to happen, and that excited your Kundalini. So your pendulum swung to the other side of Zero Point."

"Amazing..." Klarissa said, marveling at her own body. "It sucks though that I can't just make it happen. I have to either dream and wake up transformed, or cast a sex spell to stimulate the Kundalini. Or so it seems."

"I can teach you how to mentally control your Zeromorphosis," Machandi continued. "Through techniques of meditation and body movement exercises. But this will make it a lot easier. Sit in lotus pose and close your eyes." Klarissa did, getting in a meditative frame of mind. "Your Kundalini rose, but then went down again to the base of your spine. I see it now."

A ball of yellow light energy appeared rotating at the base of Klarissa's spine like a ball of coiled up snakes. "What are you going to do?" Klarissa asked.

"I'm going to raise it up and connect it permanently." She took a deep breath in her plasma-body, and since she was non-corporeal, she was able to slip her hand right through Klarissa's pelvis and grasp that bright yellow ball of energy. Klarissa could feel the tingles of electricity traveling up her spine and shooting out of her Crown Chakra. Then, pulling the ball of yellow energy up toward her head, Machandi forced it through every Chakra until she let it lock in place at the sixth Chakra—the Third Eye. The excess energy exploded out of her top Chakra and golden light rained down on her in a shower of bliss.

Klarissa finally opened her eyes and she could feel the newly awakened energy coursing through her. She felt the yellow light converging at her solar plexus, and when she looked down, she saw a yellow spiral of light flowing like liquid out of her chest. "What is that?" she asked.

Machandi smiled and replied, "That is called the Soul-mind."

# Seven

# The Center of the Dyadic Cyclone

Klarissa had been practicing the meditations as well as the Sacral Chakra and pelvic floor exercises for several days and it wasn't working to transform her. She was getting frustrated. Machandi told her not to rush the process. You can't learn a new skill overnight—especially if that skill involves transmogrifying entire body parts.

"Ah, this is useless," she griped, breaking out of her meditation and uncrossing her legs from the lotus pose she had been sitting in. "Might as well take a break. Maybe I'll go see if Lilith is at *The Chai Shop*. Would she recognize me? I wonder if she'll recognize me."

"Don't forget to keep practicing," the blue goddess said before disappearing. Klarissa needed a break from that alien anyway. It's not that she didn't like having the company, and she'd learned a lot from the Blue Fairy Godmother, but sometimes she just wanted to have some time alone without having to be ready at any moment for a Pleiadian extraterrestrial to Astral Project right next to her in the back of her van. There was no privacy with a being like that. *Maybe I need to expand the inside of* The Quantum Shortbus, *Klarissa thought. Could I do that Magickally? Maybe through some powerful Sex Magick?*

She continued to think about ways she could 'Doctor Who' the inside of her space-van as she drove back into the town of Mount Shasta. The way that her perfect spacecraft looked in her imagination was that the inside was indeterminately large. And it could reconfigure itself based on the desires of the Captain's—Klarissa's—mind. She still imagined that the outside looked the same—except for a triplet of jet-thrusters attached to the back doors.

While she was lost in her fantasy, the drive flew by and Klarissa found herself already outside of the little Chai Shop. She changed out of her sweats and into a tight t-shirt and skinny jeans. The quaint little shop never looked more open and ready for business. So she hopped out of her van/house/spaceship and then took a deep breath as she entered again into the den of sex. Shock set in when she saw a man behind the counter. She stopped and looked at him. He smiled and waved. *Friendly enough, Klarissa thought. Who is this guy?*

The young man was tall and muscular like a body builder. His wavy brown locks flowed down either side of his head all the way to his shoulders. He also had a beard that was well trimmed. "Are you...filling in for Lilith today?" Klarissa said, pointing at the man and approaching the counter.

He laughed. "No, I'm her husband."

"Husband? She didn't say anything about a husband."

"Oh, you two talked?" the husband asked.

"Just briefly," she replied hastily. "What's your name?"

"My given name is Adam," he explained, "but I go by Atomsk. And you gotta say it like that too—all dramatic. A-toe-musk!"

"That's a cool name," Klarissa commented. "Maybe I should come up with a name like that. Something dramatic and mystical."

"Are you a cosmic alien?" Atomsk said.

"No, but I'm working on it."

Atomsk laughed at the frankness of Klarissa's reply. There was sarcasm in her smile and in her eyes, but behind that there was something more; as if she was giving away her secret and only barely glossing over it with humor. "Well," Atomsk continued, "Timothy Leary said that we are all metamorphosing into space beings. That's the next stage in conscious human evolution."

"Who's Timothy Leary?" Klarissa asked, a little of her inexperience showing.

Atomsk blinked twice as if not believing his ears. "Timothy Leary," he repeated. "Timothy Leary. The psychologist who pioneered LSD research for conscious brain change. You've really never heard of him?" Klarissa shook her head. Atomsk looked her up and down, as if assessing her. "You look like someone who might be an acidhead." He smiled, trying to make it clear that the statement wasn't an insult.

Klarissa coughed out a little laugh. "So you're saying I look like a drugged out hippie? Not sure if I should take that as a compliment."

The smile on Atomsk's face faltered briefly. "No—that's...not what I meant. I just meant—since you're in this little magickal shop—you look like someone who might be into New Age stuff and mystical psychonaut consciousness research. Maybe I was being too forward," he continued. "That's something I notice that I do—act too familiar with people I've just met. Anyway, can I get you something? It's on the house."

"Uh, yeah," she responded. "I like the chai with like two shots of espresso and hemp milk."

"Hemp milk?" he said as he pulled a cup off the stack. "That's classy. Not many people order the hemp milk."

"It's my favorite," Klarissa said a little absentmindedly as she let her gaze stray to looking around the shop again. "And don't worry about the 'acidhead' comment. I can see that I might have that kind of energy. I'm a yogi and do a lot of meditating—and I also smoke a lot of weed." She looked back at Atomsk and grinned widely, showing her white teeth. "But I haven't really experimented with many other drugs."

"But are you open to exploring?" Atomsk asked with a twinkle in his eye as he put the lid onto Klarissa's chai.

"Yeah," she replied after a moment's pause. "Yeah, I think I am."

"What did you say your name was?" he asked, holding the steaming drink out over the counter toward her.

"I didn't," she said, reaching for the tea. As she went to grab the cup, their fingers touched. Suddenly there was a spark there, a rush of energy between them—sexual or spiritual, or both, Klarissa wasn't certain. "My name is Klarissa."

She took the cup from Atomsk's hand, and as she did, he remarked, "Klarissa... What a lovely name."

Klarissa took a sip of the chai and almost burned herself. "Oooh, that's hot," she said, blowing through the hole in the lid.

"Yeah, you are," Atomsk said, smiling wide again.

Klarissa felt her cheeks get flushed in spite of the corny line. She had a moment of déjà vu and thought back to when she—or he—had met Lilith. Hadn't she made a similar comment trying to hit on her-him? A chuckle escaped her lips as she thought about it. "That's why I get them iced sometimes," Klarissa explained. "Because these drinks always seem to come out too hot for me. It's okay though. I like it. It's not too scalding that I can't drink it." She blew on the hole a couple more times and sipped it tentatively as not to burn her tongue again.

After grabbing a piece of ice from the ice tray, Atomsk walked out from behind the counter and stood in front of Klarissa. He was easily a foot taller than her and she looked up at him shyly. She was definitely attracted to him and he seemed to be coming onto her, which she liked, but she hadn't much experience navigating this type of situation in her female form. "Stick out your tongue," he commanded, firmly but gently. Klarissa slowly parted her lips; he watched as they sensually glistened with saliva. *She has very kissable lips*, Atomsk thought. Her mouth opened and she slid her pink tongue a little ways out over her bottom lip. Gently he placed the ice cube onto her tongue to cool down where she had burned herself. Then he slid the ice up farther on her tongue and into her mouth. Klarissa closed her lips, taking the ice cube into her moist mouth, her lips now wrapped around Atomsk's finger. He slid it from her mouth very suggestively. "Is that better?" he asked.

She nodded, sucking on the ice cube. Taking another sip of the her chai, Klarissa let the hot liquid flow over the ice cube, cooling it down and melting the ice. As she swallowed, she felt the intense pleasure of it, enough so that she closed her eyes and gave a little moan.

"You're so cute," Atomsk said sincerely as he brushed a strand of Klarissa's hair back behind her ear.

"Atomsk..." she began, feeling her cheeks hot again with blush. "Are you hitting on me?" She smiled up at him and batted her eyelashes; she'd always wanted to do that.

He laughed and his eyes were kind. "I think the answer to that is pretty obvious," he replied. Touching her shoulder, he received a little shock as if by static electricity. As a reflex, he jerked his hand back slightly and his eyes got wide as he saw a burst of color erupt around her whole body. Klarissa's aura was glowing with the most vivid yellow like the rays of the Sun shining during a clear day over a magickal land.

"What is it? Did I do something?" Klarissa asked, looking around.

"No, angel... Klarissa," he said quietly, admiring her yellow aura. "It's your aura... Yellow... It's magnificent." She could see the reflection of the yellow light flickering in his eyes. As he reached back out to touch her, she could feel the sexual tension between them.

When Atomsk's hand touched her shoulder the second time, there was no shock, but her aura disappeared as quickly and jarringly as it had appeared. "What is it?" Klarissa asked.

"I don't see your aura anymore," Atomsk admitted. "But I can still feel it. Sometimes I only get glimpses of auras for a second. I don't see them all the time. Have you ever done any Angelic work?"

Klarissa shook her head. "What's that?"

"It's spiritual work connecting with the angels or extraterrestrial entities, whatever you want to call them," he answered. "Sometimes you can find out who your angelic guardians are."

"I'd be open to exploring that," Klarissa responded, still not looking away from Atomsk's eyes.

"I feel called to do this spiritual work with you," he continued. "I can feel quite a strong presence around you or connected to you somehow."

The feeling of the sexual tension was still hot in the air, and Klarissa had a distinct intuition that something was going to happen between them. "And your wife?" Klarissa dared to ask, even though she was thinking about when she-he had sex with Lilith without knowing she was married to this man standing before her.

Atomsk didn't take his eyes away from Klarissa's and he answered matter-of-factly. "We have an open relationship and marriage," he explained. "Now, are you open to sharing energy with me and exploring this spiritual work? If not, that's okay too. No pressure. I know we've only just met. But I am attracted to you and I want you to know it."

Hesitating, she didn't answer right away. It wasn't that she didn't want to journey and explore with this man, it was that she hadn't been with a man like this in her female form yet—except for when her friend James had raped her, and she didn't want to think about that. "I'm open," she said finally. "I'm attracted to you too."

"Good," Atomsk said, smiling. "That's all I needed to hear. I don't know why people in our society have so many hangups about everything, especially sex. If people are attracted to each other, they pretty much know it right away. How difficult is it to just be straight-forward about it? I'm not about that bullshit game. People are either open or they're not. I'm not going to waste my time chasing after people who aren't mature enough to say how they really feel. Better to get it all out there at the beginning so that we know if we can play. If not, then we know that's as far as it goes. Anyway... That's a discussion for another time."

"That's okay," Klarissa said, taking Atomsk's hand. "I agree with you. Let's play."

Walking over to the entrance door, Atomsk locked it and turned the sign around. "Come," he said and walked past Klarissa and through the curtain that led into Lilith's studio. Hurriedly she put her drink down clumsily on the counter and followed after him. "This is Lilith's little studio and temple," he said once she was through the curtain as well. "Nice, isn't it?"

The temple wasn't lit with candles this time, just the orange glow of a couple salt lamps. Klarissa nodded, making no indication that she had been there before. But she could still feel the buzz of energy from that Tarot reading she'd gotten from Lilith. There was incense burning, and the low light in the room from the salt lamps put Klarissa in a pleasant headspace. "It's beautiful," she said.

"Yeah," Atomsk replied, looking around the room with a smile. "Lilith really knows how to design the layout of a room for optimum flow of energy. Come, let's go up to the bedroom." Opening the door that led to the stairs, he went up, confident that Klarissa would follow behind him. She did, silently but buzzing with uncertainty and excitement. *Does this couple always try to seduce everyone who comes into their shop?* she wondered. *Or is it just me?*

"I feel this strong connection with you," Atomsk continued, looking over his shoulder at Klarissa as he reached the top of the stairs. "Like we've known each other or been lovers in other lives long past." He paused for a moment, thinking. "Do you believe in that kind of stuff?"

Klarissa shrugged. "I don't know," she admitted. "I haven't really had any experience with that."

"Hmm," was his response, taking her hand and leading her into the bedroom where she-he had sex with Lilith just days ago. Was it just days ago? The days were becoming more jumbled in Klarissa's mind—slightly confused about when he had been Calvin and when she had been Klarissa; and did their memories belong to them both or to each individually? She shook her head, clearing her mind of the thoughts. It wasn't the time or place to be contemplating the paradoxes of Zeromorphism. "Well, if you hang around me you might start having some past life memories." Atomsk looked over at her as they stood in front of the bed. "Are you okay?"

"Yeah. I'm good," Klarissa answered, reassuring him with a smile.

"Good. Just making sure," he responded. "I want this all to be consensual. That's very important. Wait here a moment." After going into the bathroom that was right off of the bedroom, Atomsk rummaged around in a drawer under the sink and then came back out with a small silver box. As he sat down on the edge of the bed, he opened it up. Klarissa could see little squares of paper scattered on the bottom of the small box. After licking his finger, he used the stickiness to pick up one of the squares and put it on his tongue. He stuck another one to the tip of his finger and offered it to Klarissa. "You want one?" he asked. "No pressure."

"What is it?" she asked. On the tiny square of paper was drawn a little cartoon outline of a penis, which struck Klarissa as funny.

"LSD," he answered. "I know a chemist in town who synthesizes it."

"Okay," she said suddenly. *Why the fuck not?* she thought.

"Cool." After sticking out her tongue, Atomsk placed the tab of acid onto it gently.

"Are you sure that your wife isn't going to be back any-time soon?" Klarissa was slightly worried about that. The last thing she wanted was to get into the middle of any marriage dispute.

"I'm sure," he said confidently as he patted the spot on the bed next to him, encouraging Klarissa to sit. "She's at a Teal Swan Synchronization workshop. Teal's teachings have helped us a lot, especially when it comes to strengthening relationships and communication." Klarissa was sort of getting used to hearing all these names of people she had no idea who any of them were. "Besides, I told you that we have an open marriage."

Klarissa wasn't entirely convinced. Not about Lilith being away at a workshop, but about the open marriage part. Wouldn't Lilith have mentioned that to Calvin when they were together? She wasn't entirely sure, but she was sure as shit not going to let that ruin a fun time with this beautiful man.

The lights were low in the bedroom as well, with several salt lamps sitting on top of stacks of books shedding their soft orange illumination into the room. Atomsk kicked his shoes off and then scooted up onto the bed, finally sitting up close to the headboard amidst the pillows with his legs crossed like a yogi. "Come sit across from me," he said, motioning for Klarissa to come up onto the bed. After kicking her shoes off as well, she hopped up onto the bed and sat cross-legged across from Atomsk, gazing into his eyes again. "Are you ready to do some spiritual work to connect to your angels or guardians?" he asked, taking hold of her hands.

"Yes."

"Good. Then let us begin." Pausing for a moment, he took a few deep breaths. "Continue to gaze deeply into my eyes. And I will gaze deeply into yours. This connects us Tantrically. Breathe slowly and deeply as I do. This will help synchronize our energy."

As Klarissa continued to connect with Atomsk, she could feel herself sinking into a very deep relaxation. She was opening up, the energy of her heart chakra grasping out toward him. There was a feeling of tranquil euphoria that was drifting up her spine like a pleasant breeze. Her eyelids dropped a bit, as if she was in a delightful trance, but she kept eye contact with Atomsk the whole time. After a while of the long deep breathing, Klarissa was losing her sense of time. It could have been five minutes or five hours for all she knew. And as they continued breathing, there was a sensation of becoming a wave—like they were both waves of the ocean flowing into each other back and forth, each time more of themselves became lost in the other.

"I call on the Unified Field by name," Atomsk suddenly said, not loud but in a forceful whisper. "The Unified Field which we are always connected to and part of. An indispensable piece of the fabric of creation. We can interface with this Field directly, and this ability is always available to us. We just have to ask. To speak to it. To work with it. To gain answers from it. For it to work on our behalf. Everything is always unfolding in my favor."

"Everything is always unfolding in my favor," Klarissa repeated.

"Anything that we ask of the Unified Field and the Spiralverse we can have," Atomsk continued.

Klarissa repeated again. "Anything that we ask of the Unified Field and the Spiralverse we can have."

"Repeat after me again," he continued. "I trust that the energies, the environment, and the people involved here have my best interest at heart."

She repeated these words.

"I choose to love all of existence and all of experience, beyond duality and beyond the limitations of mind."

Klarissa repeated these words as well.

Atomsk had one final affirmation. "I surrender to the medicine, and to the experience it brings."

This statement was also mirrored back to him by his Tantric partner.

"Trust. Love. Surrender," he said finally.

"Trust. Love. Surrender," she echoed back.

Klarissa had never experienced an LSD journey before, but she was definitely feeling the come-up and it seemed like she was being sucked into the void. But it was not a feeling of nothingness. It was beyond that—beyond the nothingness, beyond the all—even beyond neutrality. Klarissa didn't have sufficient concepts in her mind to describe it even to herself.

"Now we call in the guardians," Atomsk said quietly as he closed his eyes. Taking his lead, Klarissa closed her eyes as well. When she did this her skin began to tingle all over, as if ants were running around under her flesh, but it was a pleasurable sensation, almost sexual. "If Klarissa has any angels watching over her," he continued, "or extraterrestrial guardians watching over her, come commune with us now. Share your wisdom. We are friends."

Even with her eyes closed, Klarissa could feel the space of the room around her. Without even looking, she had the feeling a torrent of energy was flowing around them like a cyclone—and they were at the center of this cyclone. Calling on deities who were beyond this level of reality—beyond this Dimension, yet interacting with it all the time, invisibly.

After a while of just flowing with the energy, Atomsk opened up his eyes. His pupils were dilated to the point where his irises were just a sliver around the blackness within them. *That acid has definitely hit me*, he thought. The aura around Klarissa was visible to him again, more intense and it had expanded. The yellow tendrils were flicking out as if trying to lick the walls of the room. "I'm feeling a presence joining us here," he said, perceiving a disturbance in the air behind Klarissa and off to her left. There were waves in the air, like off a hot highway before seeing a mirage in the desert. At first these waves were just transparent, bending the air within his field of vision like he had just huffed a bunch of nitrous. Then the waves began to turn blue and flicker. Within the flash of an instant, Machandi's plasma-body form appeared within that space, a little more transparent that usual and flickering as if she was just an image on a broken television. Atomsk's mouth hung slightly open as he beheld the form of the alien goddess. "I see a guardian watching over you," he spoke. "More alien than angelic. A Pleiadian to be precise. A beautiful feminine goddess with gorgeous blue skin. She..." He stopped for a second, listening and staring at Machandi. The goddess's lips moved briefly as if she was saying something but no audible words could be heard. "She says," Atomsk continued. "That you are protected on your sacred journey. And that she is always watching out for you and assisting you as best she can."

"You can see her?" Klarissa said, slurring her words a bit as her eyes fluttered open. When her eyes were fully open and she looked back into Atomsk's, the image of Machandi flickered and disappeared out of his vision. "I wasn't sure she was real. I thought she might have only been in my imagination."

"Is there a difference?" he asked, completely sincerely.

Suddenly Klarissa caught a glimpse of something hovering above and behind Atomsk. An intense light like the light of the Sun shown down on her almost violently. She felt the reflex to shield her eyes from the intensity but she didn't. Hovering above Atomsk was the most angelic figure she had ever seen—something straight out of Greek mythology. The figure was a large man, almost a giant, and chiseled so muscular like the statue of David. His dark blonde hair was long and flowed around his shoulders along with his long beard. He was naked, with the most perfect looking cock that Klarissa had ever seen. There were huge white wings jutting out from either shoulder behind his arms which were stretched out like a cross. There was blazing fire all around him, the flames so violent that Klarissa was afraid that it might catch the whole room on fire. Suddenly flaming balls appeared in this deity's hands as well, wielding the fire like it was its duty to obey his commands.

"Holy shit," Klarissa said in a squashed little voice.

Atomsk could see the flames shimmering, reflected in her eyes. And he knew his guardian had appeared as well. "You can see him?" he asked, smiling with pleasure that both their guardians had appeared for them.

"Who is *that*?" she said. The vision of this angel was utterly terrifying. If Atomsk hadn't been there, Klarissa would have run as fast as she could alway from the creature.

"He is *my* Holy Guardian Angel," he explained. "I use Prometheus."

"Prometheus..." she repeated the name in awe, as she remembered vaguely reading something about this god somewhere along the way.

"Ask him if there is anything you need to know now," Atomsk continued.

She tried to muster up the courage inside of her even though the fear was trying to take hold. There was immense difficulty since she was inexperienced navigating all the chaos of feelings being stirred up by the LSD. Taking a deep breath, she asked, "Prometheus, is there anything I need to know now?"

Prometheus turned his head slowly to look down at her as if he was a statue carved in stone. The flames continued to blaze and lap around his head. His eyes also seemed to burn with this same fire. Klarissa could feel this entity—or deity—staring straight into her soul; if the soul indeed even existed. And she was suddenly afraid that he might call her out on her secret of being a Zeromorph, stripping her naked in front of this man she wanted to experience intimacy with. More naked than she was ready or willing to be.

"Illumination," Prometheus began in a booming voice. "Illumination is for every individual, excluding none. Even you. Illumination is your birthright." Right after he was finished with that short speech, the god pulled his arm back and hurled one of the fireballs straight at Klarissa. This intense light and heat hit her directly in the face, dissipating and then feeling like it was consuming her entire head. She gasped and it was like a sun had burst in her vision. Shaking her head and closing her eyes tightly shut, Klarissa thought she could shake the intense light loose like stardust being shed from her hair. When she opened her eyes again, still all she could see was this bright white as if a floodlight was being unceasingly illuminated into her stricken face.

Squinting her eyes against the onslaught of light particles, she tried to will the brightness to become less intense. As if yielding to her unspoken desire, the light diminished, and yet all around her still seemed to remain just white. *I must be tripping hard*, she thought. Was the hallucination that powerful and that externalized that it could transport her to another place entirely? If where she found herself even was a *place* and not just the inside of her own mind. As she looked around, the white whatever seemed to stretch out infinitely all around her. However, she wasn't sure if above her and below her stretched to infinity because she could see faintly a gray outline of a grid below, on what she seemed to be standing on, and above her on what seemed to be some kind of ceiling.

After barely enough time to register her environment, the whiteness of the space suddenly became black. And not just black—darkness. Klarissa couldn't even see herself anymore, she was swimming in the infinite darkness. But then there was illumination again. As if within the backdrop of that darkness, tiny pinpricks of light began to appear which looked like stars. Then planets began to form; and suns; and moons; and galaxies. It was like a hologram projected all around her, but with more stars and planets than she'd ever seen at a Planetarium. This multiverse—or Spiralverse—sprawled out all around her farther than she could see. This hologram even extended farther above her and below her, so far out that she couldn't see any end to it.

Several yards in front of her within her field of vision appeared a galaxy which she recognized—the Milky Way. A warm feeling of unconditional love consumed her, radiating out from her heart and sending chills and waves around her body and out into her aura. Slowly she walked through the hologram toward the image of her own galaxy. As she walked through stars, planets, nebulas, and black holes, each of these heavenly bodies felt warm and charged with immense energy as they traveled through her. Now she was right up against the spiral of the Milky Way and could see her own solar system within its midst. Earth was like a beacon of blue light, calling out to her with longing. Klarissa's yellow aura responded by pulsing and growing a foot larger around her. Then there was a tingling sensation around her heart and a spiral of yellow energy began to emanate therefrom.

She gasped, her eyes fluttering from the intensity of the feeling of ecstasy. *Is this what it feels like to make love to a god?* she thought. The sensation was as if her heart was opening up, ripping apart to let more love in. It wasn't painful, far from it. She wanted to take all of Mother Earth into herself—into her heart—and love it, all its creatures and plants and weather and environments; to cherish it forever as her home planet who nurtured her and raised her and cared for her... and loved her so much that it would die for her as she died and then raise her back to life again just to set her sights again toward the stars. So she took the planet into her heart.

With another gasp of psychedelic orgasmic ecstatic awareness, Klarissa jolted forward, ushering the hologram of the Earth into her chest through her ribcage. The yellow spiral of her Soulmind coming from her heart was like a hand and a mouth at the same time, sucking the planet into her heart. She could feel it, as her heart beat around the planet, pumping blood to her body and spiritually to Mother Earth. The tides of the ocean were like a roaring tsunami melting her and reconstituting her like a mermaid tumbling through metaphysical waves.

Closing her eyes, she focused on the sensations running through her which were intensely sexual; and it felt to her as if she was making love to the entire cosmos in that moment. Within this holographic experience she was nude and she had been since the bright white light, but she hadn't become aware of it until this moment as she rubbed her hands over her skin as it tingled. The aura of the Earth within her ribcage and between her breasts had intercourse with her own aura, making her feel like her body was an extension of the Earth—which in reality it was—and she was becoming one with it in an orgasmic conjunction. The conjugal conjunction of all heavenly bodies. Klarissa moaned again as she squeezed her breasts and teased her sensitive nipples. There were stars and other planets going down from the horizontal plane at her heart and she could feel them pleasurably up and down her abdomen, her legs and buttocks, and there were other suns teasing at the lips of her vulva. There was a tingling in her clitoris and her pussy began to drip with exquisite wetness.

She opened her eyes and suddenly had the urge to bring the Earth's Sun into their celestial copulation. Reaching out her right hand, Klarissa cupped her fingers around the hologram of the Sun. She could feel the heat and it was almost too much for her body to bear. The yellow rays of the Sun traveled up her arm like electricity and traveled through her entire being, illuminating her aura even brighter. It felt like being in a sauna, and a thin layer of sweat glistened on her sensuous flesh as she began to pant. The Moon pulsated with blue-white light as if calling out to her to connect them—the Earth, the Sun, the Moon, and her in a cosmic foursome. Klarissa obliged, knowing that the Moon's energy was cooling and would balance out the heat from the Sun. Reaching out her left hand, she cupped the hologram of the Moon.

Instantly there was a cooling sensation running up her left arm like the flow of a river. The Moon's presence in this Tantric dance balanced out the intensity of the Sun's heat, bringing the orgasmic hum down to a pleasant rage underneath her skin. The Sun and the Moon were feeding sexual energy into the Earth within her and suddenly she could feel the Earth fucking her, all the way from her pussy through her Crown Chakra. She cried out with the exquisite agony and threw her head back, feeling like her brain was going to explode with the most powerful orgasm she'd ever experienced in her life. It was like up and down from her heart she was being impaled by the hugest cock she could imagine. It was filling her up, pushing on her skin from the inside as if the force of the orgasm would rupture her entire being, shattering her into dark nebulas, stars, and galaxies. An orgasm so forceful that it could give birth to the Spiralverse and Beyond.

"Klarissa..." It was Atomsk's voice and it echoed around Klarissa's psychedelic cosmos and faded before she could even begin to register it had made a sound. "Klarissa," he said again, a little more forcefully. And this time it penetrated her consciousness before it faded into the darkness of her space.

"Uhhh," she moaned as she opened her eyes. All she could see was the cosmos hanging in the black background of space. The suns below her Milky Way were vibrating against her clitoris and she was almost so sunken into her psychosexual trance that she didn't want to come back, it felt too amazing. "I just want the heavens to make love to me forever," she mumbled, closing her eyes again and sinking back into the ecstasy.

This time, as her eyes fluttered closed, she felt a pressure on her lips—the wet skin of another's lips. Atomsk kissed her from outside of her experience, trying to bring her back. Klarissa's lips moved, accepting the kiss and inviting more. She parted her lips and as she felt Atomsk's tongue slip into her mouth, she greeted it with her own. Beginning to feel his body close to hers, she opened her eyes and was back in his room, on the bed. Atomsk's face was close to hers and their mouths were on each others, both enjoying the taste of the other.

"You brought me back," Klarissa whispered.

"Where were you?" Atomsk asked. "You looked so very far away. Or very deep into your inner world."

"I was far out in the cosmos," she replied. "Or maybe it was the Spiralverse within myself that I was experiencing."

"You can go just as far out as you're willing to go within," Atomsk said with a smile and proceeded to kiss her more. On her lips then down her cheek, and when his lips brushed her neck, she moaned with pleasure, her eyes rolling back in her head.

"You're making me so wet," Klarissa whispered as Atomsk continued to suck and nibble on the side of her neck.

"I thought the stars were making you wet," he said, moving his head away from Klarissa's neck and looking up. "Do you see them?" She looked up and suddenly pricks of starlight began to appear all over the ceiling and walls as if from a projection. Yet there was no projector; this vision was produced directly from their own consciousness. There were green waves of light energy dancing between the light of the stars.

"Wow," she uttered.

"Every man and every woman is a Star," he said, staring deeply into Klarissa's dilated eyes. She raised her arms up above her head, wanting to be undressed. Atomsk obliged, pulling her shirt up and over her head. Klarissa wasn't wearing a bra and she was a little shy about her small breasts. There was almost a reflex to cover her chest with her arms, but Atomsk gently held her wrists and guided them to her sides. Then he leaned down, kissing her chest and sucking her nipples, making them wet and erect.

Atomsk felt Klarissa pulling at his shirt as well and allowed her to slowly undress him. His chest was broad and rippling with muscle. Below his pecs were slim and toned abs. Running her hands up and down his biceps as she kissed his chest, Klarissa could feel even more wetness between her legs, soaking her panties. With grace and respect for the goddess energy, Atomsk held her shoulders and laid her down on her back. Next he was unbuttoning her pants and gently sliding them off. He threw them onto the floor and then dropped his head to kiss the sweet flesh of her thighs. The white panties Klarissa was wearing were soaked completely through and Atomsk could smell her sweet scent. It aroused him, making him feel his erection pushing against the front of his pants into the bed.

"Can I?" he asked, placing his hands on her panties on either side of her hips. Klarissa nodded and the stars spun in her vision above her. With no hesitation, but with no sense of urgency or rush, Atomsk slid her panties off and tossed them over the side of the bed. He took her socks off as well, like he was unwrapping a present that he was relishing the experience of revealing slowly just as much as if that was the gift itself. When his tongue went inside her, she gasped with the surprise. She could feel it, thick and wet, and lapping at the walls of her vagina. The pleasure instantly exploded like a supernova, and to Klarissa it felt like stars were exploding and being born all around them. She could feel every move of his tongue inside her, licking her g-spot and hitting every other pleasure zone—even ones she didn't know she had.

Moaning with the mad ecstasy, Klarissa reached down and ran her fingers through Atomsk's hair which was falling in waves around his head and pooling onto the inside of her thighs. She felt like her cunt was so voracious that it wanted to devour his entire face; keeping it for its own pleasure for all eternity. There was no indication that Atomsk was tiring. He was immensely enjoying tasting her and pleasuring her this way. She was delicious and he was in rapture. Time meant nothing in that space of cosmic bliss. The waves went on and on forever as stars burst around them. The walls rippled and billowed as if they were breathing—moaning even, along with their erotic energy. Klarissa even thought for a moment, when the euphoria seemed so intense that her skull might rupture from the orgasms, that the whole house was shaking and the energy they were building between them was so strong that it might just vibrate the whole building into splinters.

She came and came and came; not knowing whether Atomsk had been eating her out for ten minutes or ten hours. The room was a blur as she opened her eyes and her head swam with colors so vivid that she thought she was in a painting that was being created at that moment. "Oh my God!" she moaned louder. "I'm gonna cum again. Fuck! Fuck! Oh my god!" As the orgasm shot to her head and exploded in her pineal gland with all the magick contained in the Spiralverse, she could feel a gush of liquid squirt from her cunt over Atomsk's tongue and into his mouth. He swallowed it immediately, enjoying the taste of her moonflower going down his throat and glowing its magick inside him.

Atomsk smiled up at her, his mouth and chin wet with her sex fluids. "You're so luminous," he said, his eyes glazed over from their play taking them to higher levels of consciousness. "And the taste of you is delicious."

"Come to me," she said, motioning for him to come up to her. "I want to taste myself in your mouth." As he crawled up to her face, Atomsk kissed the inside of her thighs again, then her belly, and then her breasts and neck. Finally he was kissing her lips and Klarissa could taste the sweetness of her sex between their tongues. Atomsk was naked now as well, he must have slipped his pants off while he was pleasuring her orally—she hadn't even noticed. But now she could feel the girth and thickness of his hard cock against her body.

As he kissed her neck again ravenously, Klarissa opened her eyes, suddenly feeling a dizziness in her head—her Third

Eye pulsing. The stars were still all around them on the ceiling and walls. As Klarissa watched, they whirled around chaotically with no apparent pattern, swimming through the green energy waves like static on an old TV screen. Sometimes they seemed to be jumping off the walls and ceiling as if lunging at her, then going back to their erratic dance. She closed her eyes against the vision because the motion was beginning to make her feel nauseous. Atomsk licked her bottom lip and then sucked on it as her mouth hung slightly agape. The tip of his cock was now sliding between the wet and glistening lips of her labia. Then suddenly he was inside her.

"Uhhh," she cried out as his whole length and girth penetrated her cunt. She could feel every inch of it and the tip brushing right up against her cervix. A knot started to form in her stomach as he slowly started to thrust his hips. He was gentle, going slowly in and out of her, but for some reason she wasn't enjoying the sensations like she had been earlier. Atomsk was a big man and muscular, a lot broader, heavier, and taller than Klarissa's small frame. And in her altered state she could feel every pound of him on top of her as if his body was going to squash her into a puddle of blood and pussy juice. There were flashes of light and darkness that began to skip across Klarissa's imagination, and then suddenly she was seeing James's face as he raped her. It was like a grotesque caricature of his face; his smile too wide and toothy like a smear of red lipstick on the painted face of a demented clown. His eyes were huge and vibrating like they were made of wet jelly. With that image, it felt to her like she was being stabbed in the vagina by a crazed maniac and punched in the cervix like it was part of a partially deflated sex doll.

"Mmmm...mmm..." she groaned, her eyes and teeth clenched tightly shut.

Atomsk stopped his movement, noticing that something was wrong. "Are you okay?" he asked. Klarissa shook her head without opening her eyes; she was trying to beat back the fear and panic that was threatening to take her over and force her to run for her life. In an instant Atomsk pulled out of her and sat up on the bed, concern evident in his face. Touching her legs lovingly with his hands, he whispered, "Are you having a bad trip?"

The room still seemed to be spinning when Klarissa slowly opened her eyes. "I don't know," she answered honestly, tears glistening in the corners of her eyes. "Painful memories..." A sob choked its way raggedly out of her throat.

"I apologize if anything I did triggered these memories," he said as he twisted around to pull a blanket out from under the pillows at the head of the bed. "You're in a safe environment," he assured her with strength and authority in his voice. "Nothing here is going to hurt you."

With a bit of a struggle, Klarissa managed to sit up on the bed and pulled her knees into her chest. Atomsk wrapped the blanket around her shoulders to try to comfort her. "Thank you," she said. Atomsk could barely hear the words because they came out as a squeak from her dry throat.

"Just sit here and breathe for me," he continued. "I have something that will help you."

Klarissa nodded as she let her head drop between her knees. After leaving the room, Atomsk went downstairs to get whatever it was he thought could help her. Once he was gone, the sense of being alone gripped her like ice. There was an immense pain in her heart and she tried to pull her mind away from the grief attached to the memories of what had happened to her. But all she could see were her friends faces laughing with sinister smiles like they were taunting her in a circle while she lay sprawled out on the cold ground, bleeding and violated. She wailed, a scream of agony ripping from her throat like a banshee needing to be unleashed. Then the sobs shook her whole body like an earthquake, tears and snot streaming down her face.

Hearing the scream from downstairs, Atomsk was back up the stairs in a flash. Closing the door, he approached Klarissa cautiously with a glass of what looked like orange juice. She looked up as he came in the room, her face wet and almost hyperventilating from the crying. "What's that?" she managed to say.

"It's orange juice with liquid vitamin B-3 in it," he answered. "Vitamin B-3 will stop a bad trip. Will you drink it for me?" Holding out the glass to her, she slowly pulled her arm out from under the blanket and took the juice. She drank it in two gulps and handed the glass back to Atomsk who placed it on top of one of the stacks of books behind him. After sitting back down next to her on the bed he asked, "Can I hold you?"

"Please," she whispered, and without hesitation he enveloped her in his strong embrace. He put his hand comfortingly on the back of her head and laid her face against his chest. As she continued to weep, grieving for herself, for all the pain she had endured, Atomsk could feel her hot breath on his skin and then her tears.

Instead of hushing her and telling her everything was going to be all right, he said, "It's okay. Let it all out. Cry for as long as you need to. Scream if you feel like it. I'm here, you're supported and loved. Whatever you're feeling is valid and deserves full expression."

She screamed again, muffling it in his chest. Still she was violently shaking but her heart was beginning to feel like it was slowly healing, the pain she had been feeling so acutely was subsiding. Atomsk's blue aura was calm and large around his body, exuding as much vibrations of love and healing that he could send out. Klarissa's yellow aura was chaotic, like a blazing forest fire—hectic and confused. Willing his aura to move, he instructed it to meld with hers, the blue and yellow tendrils of energy beginning to flirt and dance through each other. Then both fields of energy began to braid together, allowing Klarissa's aura to slow and calm down. A spiral of blue energy also began to extend from his heart chakra, inviting her energy to join his. Cautiously, a spiral of yellow Soulmind emerged from her heart and finally connected with Atomsk's energy.

When these energies at their hearts braided together, Klarissa gasped, feeling as if shattered pieces of her heart were being put back into place, taking the pain away. This dance of blue and yellow light continued to swirl all around them, elevating their energies and bringing Klarissa out of her painful recollections. She looked up into Atomsk's face, her eyes still wet and red. "How long was I crying?" she said, her sense of time totally distorted.

"I don't know. A while," he replied. "Are you feeling better?"

"Yes," she answered. "I feel like I've shed an entire lifetime of pain." Then she leaned in and kissed him hard on the lips, the passion igniting again. Wrapping her arms around his shoulders, she ravished him with more kisses—all tongues and wet lips. He laughed and she laughed. The heaviness had been lifted.

"Do you want to be on top?" he asked. "You can be in control so your mind doesn't feel like I'm on top of you and smothering you or trapping you. I don't want you to feel in any way that I'm being aggressive."

"Yeah," Klarissa said, smiling again and feeling the buzz of sexual tension. Putting her hands on his broad chest, she pushed him back gently until he was laying on his back. The feel of his cock was stiff against her ass as she straddled his abdomen. "Oooh," she cooed as she wriggled her perky ass back against his hard-on until it was resting between her ass cheeks. As she enjoyed pawing at the muscles of his pecs, she said, "You're so fucking hot."

"So are you," Atomsk said, moving his hands up to squeeze Klarissa's ass. "So amazingly perfect. You're like an alien goddess who enjoys seducing mortal men."

"I want you to suck on my titties," she said all of a sudden.

"What?"

"Fucking suck on my tits!" she said more forcefully and grabbed Atomsk by the shoulders and pulled him up toward her. Since he was so tall, it was a bit difficult at first to guide his head down to her breast. But he managed to catch her right nipple in his mouth, sucking and licking it like it was the most delicious lollipop he'd ever tasted. "Uhhh, yeah..." Klarissa moaned loudly, throwing her head back as she pulled his face harder onto her breast. She had never experienced her nipples being so sensitive before. It was like she had clitorises on her chest, and those clitorises were somehow attached to the clitoris between the lips of her wet vulva.

Atomsk moaned too as he continued to lick and suck with his eyes closed. He was in pure ecstasy. The sensation of his warm saliva dripping from his lips and down the underside of her breast gave her chills. *Calvin's nipples were never this sensitive,* she thought. *Wait, who the fuck is Calvin?* She laughed at the absurdity of the thought. The laughter made Atomsk stop servicing her nipple and he looked up into her laughing face, her cheeks rosy red. Feeling Klarissa's enjoyment and the sheer amusement in her laughter, Atomsk couldn't help feeling elated as well. And he began to laugh. Which made Klarissa laugh all the harder; then they were both laughing at some hilarity that neither of them quite could pinpoint.

"Why are we laughing?" Atomsk said, tears of joy streaming down his face.

"I don't know," Klarissa responded. "But it feels amazing." Then without warning she grabbed his hard cock from behind her and guided it into her luscious cunt. She took him all inside her, completely and totally, grinding her clit against his pelvis. "Fuck," she groaned. "You're so thick." Her head felt so light from all the laughing that she almost thought it would float away into the stars shining from the ceiling.

"Is it okay?" Atomsk asked. "I'm not hurting you?"

"No," she replied. "I love it." Grabbing his hands, she put them on either side of her hips. The feel of her smooth skin was enough to drive anyone wild. With his hands, Atomsk guided her backwards and forwards on his cock, grinding her pussy hard against him, stimulating her clit. "God! It feels so fucking good I think my pussy is gonna gush all over you!"

"Gush all over me!" he begged. Inside of her vagina, he could feel every bit of her and every fluctuation of energy. She was so wet, and the walls of her vagina hugged his penis like a warm loving embrace. The sense of Klarissa's orgasm building was so palpable that Atomsk could feel it culminating in her clitoris and her brain. The stars and green flows of energy all around them also seemed like they were pulsing toward them, helping to edge her toward an explosive orgasm.

Then she leaned back, riding his cock and letting him get a great view of her gorgeous body. She moaned as she slid her pussy all the way up his shaft and then back down, sliding him inside her again. Then she commenced with more shallow thrusts, rocking her ass back and forth. Atomsk licked his thumb and began to use it to rub Klarissa's clit as she continued to rock on his dick. "Ohhh," she said, rolling with the moan like it was a tingle and a flow of a waterfall. "Just like that, yeah. Rub that clit! Don't stop!"

Atomsk vigorously rubbed her clitoris, feeling the orgasm mounting to an incredible height—coming right to the edge and then escalating higher. The stars were in his eyes and he watched as Klarissa's head was tilted back, her eyes closed in ecstasy, moans getting louder and louder. Suddenly her form began to transform, her skin taking on a different hue in seconds. Right before Atomsk's eyes, Klarissa turned a dark shade of blue, her head became bald, and her ears pointed. She was taking on the form of Machandi, the Pleiadian guardian that he had briefly witnessed earlier. He continued rubbing her clit—the transformation into godform really turning him on. His four fingers above his thumb touched her sexy flat stomach which was now blue. Her tits swelled to at least triple their size.

"Keep going! Keep going! Rub my clit faster!" Klarissa in Machandi's form said as she pulled her head up and looked down at Atomsk who had also undergone a transformation. Below her now was Prometheus, his eyes burning with that same fire. Klarissa's mouth hung open as she moaned and continued her motion as she took his cock inside her. The huge wings of Prometheus sprawled out on the bed under his back and there seemed to Klarissa to be a blazing fire on the floor all around them. She squeezed her pussy muscles as she rode him, teasing the sensations running through his cock.

"Uhhh, oh yeah. That feels fucking amazing," Atomsk said through Prometheus's lips.

That turned Klarissa on to no end and she suddenly felt a bolt of orgasmic electricity shoot from her clitoris straight up and into her pineal gland. "Oh, fuck, I'm gonna fucking cum soon," she groaned, her legs and pussy shuddering.

When she said this, all the stars and green fields of energy got excited and flew off of the walls and ceiling. This torrent of green and white light began to swirl around the two of them like a cyclone. They were in the eye—the eye of the I. The swirl of shooting stars and green light was a storm of bliss adding to the compounding of sexual energy charging between them. "I want you to cum! Cum for me! I want to feel your divine cunt shuddering around my cock!" spoke the lips of Prometheus but with the voice of Atomsk.

All they could see around them was a blur of white and green. Klarissa gyrated up and down harder as she rode his rock-hard cock, her legs spasming from the intensity of their supernatural lovemaking. Atomsk rubbed her clit that much harder and faster.

"Ahhh! Ahhh! Oh my God, I'm gonna cum!" she screamed.

"Cum, baby! Cum all over me!"

Klarissa screamed with the intensity of her orgasm as it ripped through her body like a crack of thunder. She could feel it bursting from her clitoris and up into her head. The feeling was so intense that she felt like her clit was going to explode and her head would split from the rapture of it. "Ahhh fuck!" she shrieked and her body shook hard as all the tension that had built up rushed out of her vagina like a dam bursting. When this happened, Klarissa gushed, squirting her fluid in a rush of splendid wetness all over her Tantric partner. In those moments the orgasm took her body like a tsunami, the cyclone of stars and green toroidal fields went berserk, sweeping through the whole room and through their bodies. As these star fields touched their bodies, their godforms dissolved, revealing their human selves again.

"Are you gonna cum too?" Klarissa asked breathily, face flushed and eyes super dilated, as she continued to thrust her dripping cunt onto his cock. As the intensity of the orgasm dissipated throughout the room, the stars and green fields returned to their places around the ceiling and walls.

"I practice semen retention," he answered, regulating his breathing, keeping it steady, long, and deep. "When I do ejaculate inside a goddess, I make sure I drink the mingling of our fluids. The Alchemists call it the Elixir of Life."

"I don't think I'm ready for that," she responded, slowing down the motion of her hips. "But I am having a wonderful experience. Whoa..." She stopped and put her hands on Atomsk's chest, blinking her eyes a few times. "I suddenly feel...very light."

There was suddenly a space between Klarissa's hands and where she had just been touching his chest. Atomsk could feel the suction of her pussy pulling up the shaft of his cock. Within a few moments, her body had decoupled from him and she was floating up toward the ceiling as if all the gravity had been sucked out of the room. "Whoa," Atomsk said, reiterating the sentiment. "This has never happened to me before. This is trippy." Just as he said this, his body began floating off of the bed as well. It was as if they had become two nude astronauts floating around a space station. Atomsk flipped around until he was floating horizontal like Superman flying through the sky. Reaching out for Klarissa as she began to float away toward the wall, he grabbed one of her hands and then the other. They were weightless, holding hands like two skydivers, and began to spin lazily like a propeller blown by the wind.

They began to laugh, enjoying the sensation. Floating as if weightless had served to heighten their elation even more. "I feel like an astronaut in space," Klarissa commented. "And we are the only two people floating like cosmic lovers through an endless sea of stars."

"Me too," Atomsk said, staring deep into the blackness of her eyes; feeling as if the chaos of the void or abyss therein would devour him. "I feel like no matter how far out you journey into the expanse, that we would always become intertwined again like we were two atoms engaged in quantum entanglement."

Suddenly and without warning Atomsk let go of Klarissa's hands. She cried out with surprise as they both started to float backwards toward opposite walls. When their feet touched the wall of stars, they pushed off like swimmers in an olympic pool. Now they were playing, spinning through space and floating around each other, synchronizing and dancing through the altered spaces. They continued to laugh with joy as they performed their weightless Tantric dance, very much loving the feeling of flying, like they were two majestic birds acting out an elaborate mating ritual in flight.

As they tumbled through the air with and around each other, trails from the light of their auras were left in their wakes. Spinning patterns of blue and yellow painted through the air in psychedelic patterns becoming beautiful swirls of living music and vibration. They were in each other's energy—they were *sharing* each other's energy. Their energies were making love, as if one integrated Soulmind was being created out of their Sex Magick, more powerful and inexplicable than either one was separately.

"I wonder how astronauts have sex in zero gravity?" Klarissa asked as they floated slowly toward each other once again.

"Let's find out," Atomsk returned as they collided like two planets caught in each other's gravitational pull. They wrapped their arms around each other, kissing again as they spun in the air. Klarissa put her legs around his waist as they explored each other's mouths with their tongues. The sexual energy was still thick in the air like charged electricity and Atomsk was already erect again. The feeling of his hard cock against her ass was pleasant, turning her on even more. She was still incredibly wet and it wasn't difficult for him to slide back inside now that they were locked together in a floating embrace.

For a while they just floated there, still, joined together as lovers do. Their mouths were pressed together, lips to lips, but they had frozen, enjoying and leaning in to the sensation of melting into each other; like it wasn't just him inside of her, but she was also inside of him. They were the Divine Androgyne—the Beast with Two Backs. The blue and yellow light of their auras continued to dance around them and braid together into a conjoined energy of Love. With her eyes closed, Klarissa could see an image of Atomsk's body as if his skin was transparent. She saw his Energy Body, his Subtle Body. Even though there were blue fames of light all around him, Klarissa could perceive a tangle of light tentacles at the base of his spine, writhing together like a pit of snakes.

Finally breaking into motion after a long while of looking like a sculpture based on a passage from *The Kama Sutra*, Klarissa moved her left hand down to Atomsk's lower lumbar, right above his ass crack. Then her fingers sunk into his flesh. He cried out, moaning with a sound somewhere between pain and ecstasy. In the flash of an instant, Klarissa's hand was around his Kundalini coiled at the base of his spine. The sensation strangely did feel like hundreds of tiny snakes slithering around her fingers which were gripping this energy like an electrified ball.

"W-what are you doing?" Atomsk asked. He could barely speak and his eyes were rolling back up into his skull like he was falling into a trance.

"Shhh..." she shushed him as she began to pull the ball of blue energy up his spine. It was like she was tearing it through his spine and Chakra System but connecting it up his central vertical column as she went. Atomsk's spine began to illuminate with the blue light as Klarissa continued to move it up toward his head. Finally she pulled the energy up past his neck and connected it into his pineal gland—his Third Eye. With that connection there was a tremendous burst of energy and power which shot through Atomsk's body then out and around the crown of his head. He let out a loud cry as if he was having a huge orgasm. The blue light exploded again through his pineal gland and shot out sparkles around his head which rained down all around them like pixie dust.

The power of the energy blast forced Klarissa to pull her hand out of his head. The force of the aftershock pulsed back through her arm sending blue waves of his Soulmind into her body and electromagnetic field. Their Soulminds were now communicating, coming online, and stretching out into the Unified Field to put in motion events neither of them were even yet aware of. Opening his eyes slowly, Atomsk looked into the face of his new lover. "That felt like I had the most intense orgasm but it was in my brain," he said. "What did you do?"

"I don't really know," she answered. "It was like something took over me. I pulled your Kundalini energy up your spine and connected it so your Soulmind could link up."

"Soulmind..." he echoed back. It wasn't a question; it was just his way of validating her, mirroring her reality so that it could be real—or become that much more real. "I feel like we've journeyed all the way to the outer limits of the Spiralverse and the cosmos," he continued. "And we arrived to find ourselves home again. In each other's arms."

As he spoke these words, their weight started to return and they began to float back down toward the bed, still coupled together. Floating down, Klarissa was on top of Atomsk again and eventually he came to rest on his back on the bed once more. They both let out a deep sigh and Klarissa flopped forward until she way laying on Atomsk's chest, her face pressed against the side of his neck. He was still inside of her and he could feel his cock pulsating as her pussy squeezed around his girth. "That was amazing," Klarissa breathed, her warm breath puffing pleasantly against his neck.

"Yes. It was otherworldly," Atomsk agreed as he wrapped his arms around Klarissa's back, hugging her gently into his warm body. The stars and green fields on the ceiling and walls had calmed and now faded, the room returning to normal with just the orange glow of the salt lamps. Their respective blue and yellow auras slowed their dance and then disappeared back into themselves. It didn't all just fizzle out, though; the glow of the acid and their sex still buzzed in them and around them. "Are you an alien?" he continued, his words sounded echoey and far away. "Did you abduct me and take me to your spaceship?"

*Spaceship?* Klarissa thought, opening her eyes. It made her think of *The Quantum Shortbus* still parked outside. After kissing his neck, she rolled herself off of him to the side of the bed. "Uhhh," he moaned from the sensation of her pussy sliding off of his cock. It was pretty flaccid again, but Klarissa thought to herself how beautiful it looked glistening with her juices. "What time is it?" she asked. "That felt like an eternity and a moment, and then the flash of an instant into infinity. But as if only a second has gone by in the life of the Spiralverse."

"I know what you mean," Atomsk said. "I don't know, but it must be nighttime now. Time has a much different feel in the altered state. Are you okay?"

"I feel wonderful," she replied as she sat up on the edge of the bed and began to look for her clothes on the floor.

"Where are you going?" he wanted to know, but he made no move to stop her.

"I want to get back to my campsite for the night," she answered as she put on her panties and then pulled her pants on.

"I mean," he started, "you can stay here tonight. I don't mind. Lilith won't be home. And besides, I don't think you should drive on the medicine." He paused as she looked down at him with a loving smile. Standing there with just a pair of jeans on and topless, Atomsk thought that he'd never seen a more beautiful creature in his life. She was radiant, her skin glowing with some celestial vitality. "Then again, I'm not going to try to make you stay if that's what you want. Just be careful if you're gonna drive."

"Thank you," Klarissa said genuinely as she leaned down to kiss Atomsk on the lips. Her small breasts hung down and brushed against his chest. "I need to be out in nature right now. This whole experience—and you—have been amazing. Like nothing I've ever felt before."

"Me too," he said. "I know I'll be buzzing all night long thinking about you."

Grabbing her shirt from the floor, she pulled it over her head and then smiled again at Atomsk. "Till next we meet," she said.

"Till next time our atoms entangle," he said, giving her a wink. "Be safe."

The drive back to the campsite was slow going. Back roads into the forest weren't lit with streetlights and Klarissa didn't want to risk getting pulled over or accidentally drive off of the road. There was almost no other cars on the road, it was pretty late. However, at one point there was a car driving in the opposite direction and as it got closer to *The Quantum Shortbus*, Klarissa could have sworn that the car floated up off of the street and flew away into the night sky. She was so distracted by the flying car that she turned her head to look out the window as it floated away. Then she snapped back to watching the road, swerving slightly to get back into her lane. The road started wobbling and then it became a wave.

"Man, I am trippin' hard," she said. "Good thing I'm almost back." The road underneath the van was still waving when she pulled off onto a dirt road and drove through the trees to her campsite. The trees around her were breathing heavily, shrinking and then puffing up. And she almost thought she could hear them moaning as if there was an energetic tree orgy going on. After parking and turning the vehicle off, she sighed with relief that she didn't have to think about operating a machine anymore tonight. It was chilly, the Fall air was brisk so she crawled into the back and dug around through her clothes for a coat.

Klarissa found a long wool coat and wrapped it around her before stumbling out into the open air. Almost tripping over her own feet, she began to laugh hysterically. What was so funny she wasn't quite sure. Maybe it was her own clumsiness or just the absurdity of the situation and the day that had preceded it. She kicked the door of *The Quantum Shortbus* closed and then stood there in the middle of the campsite regaining her balance and her breath. The cool air felt good going through her nose and into her lungs, then she exhaled out of her mouth with a deep sigh. She watched the trees around her as they continued to breathe along with her. They vibrated and seemed to be shedding shiny silver sparkles. A smile pulled at the corner of Klarissa's mouth; she was still feeling high as a kite and it would come in waves of visions and euphoria.

The forest called out to her in various voices. So Klarissa began to walk away from the campsite into the trees, but making sure she didn't get too far that she didn't know where her van was parked. In her altered state, the singing of the crickets seemed louder by several degrees. The chirping seemed to be serenading her as she walked toward a little clearing in the trees. "A fairy circle," she whispered. When she said this she thought she could hear giggling of the Wee Folk and fairies that lived in these woods. Little wings seemed to fly through the trees, trailing the silver sparkles that continued to shed from the branches.

Once she got into the middle of the fairy circle, Klarissa looked up into the sky, marveling at the stars. For a moment the twinkling of the sky of stars took on the pattern and look of computer chips—or a motherboard. There were lines of electricity running in strange patterns between the stars. This made Klarissa feel like she was in a gigantic computer program where the cosmos was the main hardware and she was just one software program working in this vast network. She put her hand up and swiped her hand across the sky, making the stars go back to how they normally looked, tiny pinpoints of light—uncountable and unfathomable. In that moment the whole Spiralverse belonged to her, and the cosmos beyond it, however far out it went. To explore the outer reaches of existence would be a trip of a lifetime—or many lifetimes. *Could I be in one of those lifetimes?* she wondered. *Which lifetime am I in? Who or what am I? Am I the same in all of them? Or am I different even now? Fluxing...*

"I want to explore out there," she said out loud, looking up into space. "Are the galaxies and universes all already what they are and what they'll be, no more? Or are there new ones to be formed?" She went silent for a moment and then dropped her face to look down at her own body. Putting her hand to her chest she continued, "And I want to explore the innards of my own heart. Are the passages within it as infinite as the cosmos? As diverse? As complicated?" Then she was back looking up at the stars. "I want to create new neural pathways, new pathways of loving...new worlds to explore. And new ways of unique expression."

Suddenly the vision of the cosmos she was viewing became multi-dimensional. It was like she could view all of its different facets at once. Part of her was still viewing it from below, from her finite form. Part of her was in it—*was* it. She was every heavenly body and the Unified Field that connected everything. It was unexplainable but she could perceive the tiniest particle in a planet or a star, or she could be zoomed out, beholding an entire nebula as if hovering incorporeally in space as a vast field of consciousness. Then her arms began to move, almost involuntarily, like she was conducting an orchestra. She was conducting the galaxies. In this vision she was utilizing the basic building blocks available in space to build new structures; pulling space dust, and asteroids, and gases from stars and dying stars. Klarissa, as if a cosmic architect, was constructing new planets, new systems, new galaxies, and entire nebulas. Maybe the galaxies were shrouded in mystery by the nebulas, like an adventure to be unveiled. She was just as much discovering these new structures as she was creating them. Exploring them would be a different matter entirely.

As she continued this Pan-Dimensional art project, Klarissa felt her body transforming again. There was definitely a penis growing out between her legs, but she didn't feel any testicles descend underneath it. She thought that she might be Zeromorphing back into a man, but no, the metamorphosis was not quite that dramatic. The vagina didn't close up like it normally would have with going back to male form. And her breasts only slightly diminished. They were almost flat against her chest now, but they were still there. That was the extent of the transformation and they held that form, feeling the difference of it, as they continued to stare into the sky and pull pieces of the Cosmic Chaos together.

"Building galaxies again?"

The voice startled them out of their trance with the stars and they jumped a little before realizing it was Machandi. "Don't scare me like that," the New Creature said. "My demiurge was awakening from its slumber."

"I can see that," Machandi replied. It looked like her plasma-body was glowing blue in the Moon and star light. "Maybe you'll get to explore those worlds some day. The future is closer than you think," she said, looking up into the heavens and admiring the New Creature's handiwork.

"But how to get there, you know," they replied. "Exploring the inner worlds is much easier than finding a way to explore those far out outer worlds."

"I think you'd be surprised that that's not always how things work," Machandi commented. "For some, the prospect of exploring their inner worlds is so terrifying that they'd rather end up as a dead astronaut floating through space after the destruction of their space station."

"My space station would be indestructible," they replied confidently.

"I can tell that you've Zeromorphed again," Machandi observed.

"It seems I have," the New Creature confirmed as they slid a hand into their pants to make sure it wasn't a hallucination. There was a penis, their hand found that easily, then below that was no testicles but the opening of their vagina was still there, just the same as when Klarissa was making love with Atomsk. They pulled their hand out of their pants and licked their fingers, tasting the flavor of their own sex. "I really feel more me like this. More integrated. Who is Calvin and who is Klarissa? I don't really know who they are separately, but together, that's me... I don't know. It still doesn't make sense to me."

"It could be more of your 'true' form, if you can even call it that," Machandi said. "The fragments creating a cohesive whole maybe. But can you maintain that form? That's the real question." The New Creature smirked at this, turning their attention back toward the stars. Continuing their synthesis of new galaxies, the New Creature waved their arms wildly as if grabbing a planet from over here and pulling moons in from over there. The blue Pleiadian extraterrestrial watched with mild amusement—or was it amazement?

"Yeah, well," the New Creature interjected without ceasing their activity in the cosmos, "you could tell me how to maintain this form I hold now instead of being so fucking cryptic."

Machandi didn't say anything. Maybe she wasn't so sure herself. It was not like there was a manual for being a Zeromorph, they were still relatively rare across the Spiralverse and beyond. Maybe the New Creature was being a little unfair though; Machandi *had* been helping them, teaching them techniques, meditation, and yoga to help navigate what kind of being they were. As an alien, they probably expected her to know more than she was telling. And as the imagined 'Blue Fairy,' the New Creature maybe expected there to be some sort of Magick Wand that she could wave to fully integrate them, unlock all the powers of their Soul-mind, and give them full control of their Zeromorphic capacities. But Machandi didn't have that, and things weren't that simple. This New Creature before her was almost as much a mystery to her as they were to themself—or selves.

Suddenly the New Creature—who was as yet nameless—became illuminated by an orange light as if from the Sun, but there was no source. This light just covered their whole body and leaked out into their bio-field as if they *were* the Sun. As she watched, Machandi could tell they were oblivious to this phenomenon since they continued to build galaxies in the heavens. Machandi was the only witness to this spectacle. Within this field of orange light, the New Creature began to visually change into different forms, different characters, different people throughout history. At once they were an old Shaman, dressed like a Native American. Then they were a Russian princess in a long flowing dress. Then they were a homeless man begging on the streets of New York. Then they were a woman in a spacesuit, an astronaut floating above a space shuttle. Then they were a cult leader, speaking to multitudes. They were a general from battles long past. They were Joan of Arc. They were George Washington and then a female yogi dressed all in white with a turban wrapped around her head. How many iterations of this took place, Machandi did not know. It was like all lifetimes and identities were shown as one Soul or Spirit changing forms like clothing. The last form that Machandi witnessed the New Creature take was herself as if looking in a mirror. She saw her blue skin shining within that orange glow as the New Creature looked up into the heavens with her own face. The vision was beautiful, celestial, with the arms of this other her reaching up toward the stars. The long blue dress flowed down her slender curves and billowed wildly in some otherworldly wind.

As she watched, she looked at the pointy ears on this other-her and then studied the outline of her bald head with her eyes. Suddenly something new appeared there on top of this head. It was also blue, and at first it was too transparent for Machandi to make out. Then this thing on the New Creature-as-Machandi's head became opaque enough for her to see. It was fleshy and bulbous and moved up and down as if sucking on the scalp it was resting on. It was an octopus with large eyes that seemed wild and cartoonish. It's tentacles wriggled down the sides of the head like living dreadlocks, its suckers groping for the naked skin.

The New Creature let out a great sigh and let their arms drop to their sides as if exhausted from building galaxies for all eternity. As their blue arms swung down, the orange light melted away like liquid draining into the ground. And this melting took the image of Machandi's double with it, leaving the New Creature standing there, again an amalgamation of Calvin and Klarissa. Looking back over at their blue semi-transparent companion, they gave her a tired smile. "Thank you for witnessing me in that—whatever that was. The stages of creation or becoming or whatever the fuck. I don't even know anymore. Everything I thought I knew has come crumbling down around me like a shower of shooting stars. Even every concept I've ever had of myself has collapsed. You could just tell me who I am." The New Creature reached out their hands as if to grab something from the air. "I just can't grasp it." After a few seconds they gave up trying to hold the air in their hands and just shrugged.

Machandi smiled back at her strange companion. "See you soon, space being," she said, and then vanished.

The New Creature laughed again at the absurdity of life, or at least the life that they found themself in. The trees were still breathing and silver sparkles continued to float through the air. Their head was still buzzing from the whole experience, but could feel the exhaustion in their body. So the New Creature made their way back to *The Quantum Shortbus* and went inside as if it was their little home on wheels—which it was. They yawned as they spread out blankets on the fold-down bed in the back of the van. After plumping several pillows that they were about to lay upon, they stripped off all their clothes and flopped down on the warm blankets, sinking their head into the soft pillows.

Lazily the New Creature began to touch themself, stroking their breasts and then feeling their penis semi-hard. They flopped the penis to the side and slid two fingers into their pussy, stroking it to get it wet again and then rubbing the clitoris a bit. With eyes closed, they could still feel the buzzing of their skin from the LSD and the music of the crickets continued to sing their lullaby. Then they curled the not fully hard cock forward and under, sliding it into their own vagina. They moaned loudly. It was the most intense pleasure they'd ever felt. The sexual ecstasy could be felt building in the penis as well as in the vagina. "Uhh, my God..." they groaned as their own dick twitched inside their own cunt. The New Creature could feel their clitoris buzzing and more lubricant began to gush around their curled dick.

They knew the orgasm was going to be intense and it was building incredibly fast. Rubbing the tip of the penis inside the vagina with one hand, they used the other to stimulate their clitoris. "Yes! Yes! Oh fuck!" They screamed. "I'm gonna fucking cum! Aaagghhhh!" They screamed so loud as the orgasm ripped through their androgynous body, their eyes rolling upwards. Semen squirted in several spirts and they could feel it wet and warm as it shot back up into their own body. The orgasm was simultaneously from their cock and in their clitoris. Their legs quivered with the intensity, and the glow of euphoria remained vibrating through their whole being. After letting out a long exhale, the New Creature let their arms fall down at their sides and their penis slipped out of the dripping vagina. Their own cum leaked out bit by bit from between the lips of their vulva and it glowed brightly as if with some Elysian bioluminescence.

# Eight

## Alchemical Adversity

"Holy fucking starfish!" Calvin exclaimed as he woke up out of the deepest sleep. He felt like his consciousness had been in some deep recesses of his body and was pulled up out of some deep abyss to fill his body again. Everything around him in the van was shimmering as if it was not quite solid. The aftereffects of the acid. Right away Calvin knew he was a man again; there was pain from a full bladder that needed to be emptied and his hard-on raged from it. As he felt his balls slap against his taint, he could also feel that the vagina that had been there the night before had closed up and sealed itself back into himself.

Yawning loudly, Calvin scratched his head and could tell that his hair was frizzing and sticking up in all different directions—the ultimate bedhead. Without being quite sure his legs could carry him, he made his way with some difficulty out of *The Quantum Shortbus* so he could drain his very full bladder. With his dick still out and a few drops of piss still dripping from the tip, he squinted his eyes against the Sun that was high overhead. It definitely wasn't morning. He must have been out hard in the deepest sleep for half a day—or maybe a whole day. The thought crossed his mind that he could just check his phone to see what day and time it was, but somehow that seemed to be the least important thing in that moment.

Even though it was later in the day, it was still cold Fall weather and Calvin was butt-ass naked standing in the middle of the woods with his bare feet crunching against the leaves on the ground. Shivering as his boner went soft and shrunk toward his body for warmth, he darted back into the van to wrap himself up in a blanket. As he laid there, he went back over the jumbled memories of the chaotic, passionate, and mystical experience of the day before. With only male genitalia between his legs, he seemed to be *he*—Calvin—at the moment, and he almost grieved in his heart at the absence of Klarissa. The identity of Calvin seemed to be becoming more and more foreign to the synthesis of whoever else they were aspiring to be.

If he was to have a penis, he wanted to have a pussy too. Calvin recalled the night before briefly Zeromorphing into a full hermaphrodite, embodying the qualities of both male and female; and yet somehow transcending on either side into something more. *I want to be that*, Calvin thought to himself, pouting a little at the fact that he was back to his male form in which he felt the least comfortable in. "Why can't I fucking do what Machandi has been teaching me and transform at will already?" he said out loud. "I should be able to do this by now." Opening the blanket he had wrapped around him, he looked down at his dick. "Change, damn you." There was no response from his flaccid cock. It might have twitched a little. "Ugggh," he groaned in frustration. "What's the point of having this Soulmind whatever if I can't just command it and have it do what I say?"

In a outburst of anger Calvin smacked his nutsack as if it was the testicles' fault that he wasn't a woman. He grimaced at the pain that shot up through his pelvis like an electric shock. Trying to regain his composure and a small modicum of control, he got into a cross-legged position in preparation to meditate. The blanket draped around his shoulders like a cloak and he brushed his messy hair back out of his face. He closed his eyes and took a deep breath. Then he started to do the Breath of Fire, vigorously pumping his navel and breathing through his nose. After keeping that up for a few minutes his yellow Soulmind began to shine around his body like the aura of the Sun. Then Calvin took a deep breath and held it at the top, squeezing Root Lock; which consisted of contracting the anus, sex organs, and navel. This forced his Soulmind, or Kundalini, to travel up his spine in an uncoiling of yellow energy to illuminate his Third Eye.

Once a burst of this Soulmind light exploded in his pineal gland, he had a vision of the inner workings of his body. He could see the entire central nervous system, his organs, and his blood vessels pumping. All the neurons in his brain lit up like a switchboard. Then he began to visualize his body transforming into a female configuration. By sheer will he would make it happen—or so he hoped. There suddenly was the sensation of *something* happening in his pelvic region. He could feel his penis retracting into his body. In his visualization, as the vagina opened up between his legs, his testicles were pulled up and into his abdomen, dissolving into the lips of the labia and then traveling inside and up to become the ovaries. Calvin could feel this begin to happen. It was as if his ballsack was being pulled into his taint, melting into him. Then he lost it.

A huge sigh escaped Calvin's lips as the visualization escaped from his imagination. Letting his eyes flutter open, he looked down and saw his penis grow back out from his pubic hair and his balls dropped even lower. The opening of the vagina hadn't even started.

"Fuck!" Calvin yelled and flopped down on his back on the bed. He kicked the wall of *The Quantum Shortbus* in frustration. "Son of a motherfucking cocksucking asshole!" he cursed, grumbling that he wasn't able to make his Zeromorph work on command. "Stupid dick and balls," he whined.

Sensing Calvin's distress, Machandi appeared in her plasma-body next to the fold-down bed and sat cross-legged on the floor of the van. "I sensed your frustration," she said with concern. "Are you okay?"

"No, I'm not fucking okay," Calvin replied without looking at the alien and kicked the bottom of his foot against the wall again. "I was just getting comfortable and used to being a woman—being Klarissa. Now I'm all...*this*. I've been doing all those goddamn meditations and yoga and exercises you taught me but I still can't fucking control my transitions."

Machandi frowned, but her eyes were full of love and empathy. "That's why I said be patient. The ability will mature when it's time. You have to work it out like a muscle. You don't expect to get a six pack from doing only a week of crunches, do you?"

"Uggghh," he groaned. "Maybe I'll just go to sleep again and wake up as Klarissa. It worked before." Machandi didn't say anything. Calvin turned his head to look at her in case she was going to comment. "What?" he said when she remained silent. "Do you think that's a cop out? Do I need to try harder with the yoga?"

"Why do you need so badly to have control over this?" Machandi asked.

Calvin blinked, stunned by the question. "The fuck you mean?" he spat back. "Wasn't that the whole point of teaching me these techniques? So I can control the Zeromorphosis instead of being jerked around by it?"

"In a way that is the point. Yes," she conceded. "However it is also meant to teach you something."

"Teach me what?"

"Who are you right now?" Machandi asked.

Calvin stared at her again like he couldn't believe the words that were coming out of her mouth. "Do you not see this dick?" he said, flopping his genitals up and down.

"And?" she asked, trying to get him to see the obvious.

"I'm Calvin," he said, exasperated. "The boring dick that wants to be a vagina."

"Does that thing between your legs dictate your identity?" Machandi continued, trying to provoke some deeper thought.

"Well... Yeah," he responded honestly.

The Pleiadian shook her head. "So what you're telling me is that when you think you're Calvin, in male form, that Klarissa is not in there anywhere. That she's just gone. Where is she?"

"I don't know," Calvin sputtered. "All I know is that I don't feel how I want to feel. My body doesn't match what I am inside."

"So you're saying," Machandi continued, "that when Calvin is on the outside then Klarissa is on the inside. On the other side of the coin, is Calvin on the inside when Klarissa is on the outside?"

He sighed heavily, growing weary of this conversation. "What are you getting at, Machandi?"

"I'm just trying to get you to think about who you *really* are," she said. "Does your gender dictate who you are, or are you you no matter what? Is it your physical structure which determines it or is it something deeper? Is your true identity female or is it male? Who are you *beyond* all this gender bullshit?"

"My gender is who I am!" he yelled at her. "Without it I'm nothing! I don't want to *be* Calvin. I want to be Klarissa! I can't make myself into what I see in my mind!" Then he began to cry; sobbing because in that moment he didn't know who he was. His image of self hadn't gone deeper than the skin yet. And he felt powerless, like the control of what he wished to be was not in his hands. He had gotten glimpses of it—lived in that skin—but he couldn't hold on to it. So now he felt even more like this male body was being forced on him.

"What you're feeling is completely understandable," Machandi assured him. "I'm not trying to say that it isn't. I'm just trying to get you to look at the whole thing from a different angle. Trying to get you to see that you are more than what genitals you have. Just try to observe yourself and being a Zeromorph from more than one perspective."

"What the fuck do you know about different perspectives?" Calvin lashed out in anger as he wiped the snot running down his nose. "You've always been one thing!"

Machandi considered herself to be many things, but she wasn't going to contradict him in his angry and confused state. "I know you're angry right now," she said in a kind voice. "And I know being a Zeromorph can be highly confusing. It's normal to not really know who you are when your body is changing so rapidly and unexpectedly. Something that I think would help would be to see some other points-of-view. Try to pull yourself out of your own reality tunnel and take in some other people's perspectives."

"Oh, yeah? How am I supposed to do that?" he asked indignantly.

"I'd suggest picking up some books and read more," she explained. "Go back to that Chai Shop and see what books jump out at you. You might be surprised what you could learn. And maybe learn about yourself from reading about the experiences of others."

"Books? Are you fucking kidding me?" Calvin was yelling again. "I'm having an identity crisis and you tell me to go read a fucking book?" The rage inside of him was boiling over and he felt so frustrated that he didn't know how to get that energy out of him. He punched the inside of the van a couple times. Not hard enough to break the wall, but hard enough for it to be loud.

Machandi cringed. She hadn't meant to get him this upset. It was apparent that his inner turmoil was churning like a violent storm. "Calvin, calm down. It's not the end of the world," she said.

"Calvin! Calvin! Calvin," he repeated the name in a mocking tone. "That's not my fucking name! That's not my fucking name!" He turned to look at Machandi who he could barely see now in the low light as the Sun was going down. "You say you're helping me. You're not! You said you could help me control it. Well, I can't! You lied!"

"You'll be able to—" she started but Calvin cut her off.

"Fuck off! Get the fuck out of here! Leave me alone!" he yelled. The last few words were choked out in a sob. Then he threw himself down onto his pillow, wailing and crying into it hysterically. Machandi wished she could do more, but she knew she wouldn't be able to in that moment; Calvin was too overwrought with emotion. So his Pleiadian Guardian disappeared from *The Quantum Shortbus*, leaving her companion to work through his feelings on his own for now.

The crickets chirped out their night song but Calvin couldn't hear it. He had exhausted himself crying and then, utterly spent, fell asleep curled in a fetal position with the blanket wrapped around his body like an egg. Machandi had meant well and her intention was to provoke critical thinking, but Calvin had obviously been too emotional to process what she was trying get across. It was quite apparent that he needed to rest, but his sleep was far from tranquil. In spite of the cool night air Calvin was sweating like he had a fever. And his breathing was erratic as he tossed and turned; the protective egg of the blanket becoming a tangled mess around his thin body.

Inside his head the dreams were torturous. Even in the imagination the pain felt real in his physical body. In the nightmare Calvin was restrained on a metal slab and there were strange beings huddled all around him. These beings looked like the grey aliens that he had seen in creepy sci-fi movies, but they were taller and their bodies were fuller, more human. These Greys had long thin faces and their eyes were large and black, and to Calvin, as he stared into these eyes, they seemed to become an amorphous jelly-like abyss. He wasn't quite sure what they were doing to him, but it seemed like they were studying him and experimenting on him. The Greys moved around jerkily like their movements 'skipped' so there wasn't a continuous flow of movement. They were poking him and putting things into his body. Calvin could feel sharp pains like they were stabbing him with needles. The most uncomfortable sensations were when he could feel metal objects being inserted into his anus and urethra.

There was a scream that wanted to break free from his throat but he was gagged and his whole body felt paralyzed. However, he could move his eyes and he shut them tight. As he tried to will himself to wake from the dream, he held the image of Machandi in his mind, saying her name silently in his consciousness. This act, like a prayer to the Unified Field, was miraculously enough to pull Calvin out of the nightmare. And he awoke inside *The Quantum Shortbus*, soaked in sweat and breathing heavily.

At first he didn't remember where he was and there was still a feeling of something metal penetrating his anus as if he had taken the probe with him out of the dream. As he started to put back together his normal reality, his hands went to feel his asshole to see if something was really inside violating him. There was nothing there and the feeling quickly subsided. While his hands were down between his legs, he noticed that he still had a dick and balls hanging there. He groaned with overwhelming despondency. The hope that he would wake up having transformed into Klarissa again was crushed by the reality of his flopping genitals. "Why can't my body just change when I want it to?" he grumbled. "This is bullshit!" he whined and kicked his legs up and down on the bed.

He felt ridiculous, but that didn't make his desires any less real. The fact was that he had lived almost all of his life in a male body, as Calvin. Why was it such a hardship for him currently? Maybe because now he knew that being Klarissa, a woman, was an actuality that could manifest into physical existence, and he could live in that skin. It was painful to go back to being Calvin. He—*she*—didn't see herself that way anymore. But why? Why did that little thing have so much control over their wellbeing? Calvin didn't really have an answer for that.

Staring out of the back window of *The Quantum Shortbus* was all he could do for several minutes. His mood was definitely low and he wished that he could just float away into some alternate reality. The apathy was palpable and he just didn't feel like doing shit, even though deep down something was telling him that control of the Zeromorphosis was almost in his grasp. He knew he should be practicing the Tantric yoga and meditations, but he couldn't motivate himself in that moment.

Instead he found his pipe and the weed that he had stashed. After getting thoroughly baked, Calvin decided he should at least eat something. He felt really dehydrated so he opened a bottle of water and downed it in one go. Then he found a can of soup that he opened and ate slowly, staring off into the distance at nothing in particular. It was like he wasn't even there. Calvin wasn't who he wanted to be in that moment, so he spaced out, dissociating from that identity. And in this way, he let the day drift away like an abandoned ship on the tides of the ocean.

# Nine

## Secret Gnosis

The door of the heart pulled Calvin back into the waking world. He was reluctant to leave his dream because in this dream she was Klarissa. She was Klarissa dancing in the stars—the Cosmic Dancer in vivid rapture with the Spiralverse spinning out from her dress as she twirled through the cosmos. This dream of reverie began to fade as Calvin was coming back to consciousness of the morning in the forest by Mount Shasta. In this liminal space between waking and sleeping he wondered if since he was dreaming of being Klarissa, was Klarissa dreaming of being Calvin when he was awake?

These musings disappeared as he yawned and hoped beyond hope that during the night his body had Zeromorphed into its female form and she would once again be Klarissa in the waking world. This was not to be, he realized, when he was greeted by a raging hard-on between his legs. "Good morning, dickhead," Calvin said as he flicked the head of his penis. How many days had he been Calvin now? Several, he suspected; the days seemed to be running together in a blur like the colors of a painting in a rain storm. There was even a moment when he wondered if his body had fixed itself into male form and he would never be Klarissa again. But he didn't want to entertain that thought so he pushed it from his mind like a discarded piece of refuse that wasn't even worth a second of his attention.

Surprisingly, he felt horny. Frowning at his dick like a foreign object, he tentatively wrapped his fingers around it and began to stroke. Calvin let out a soft moan as he pleasured himself. Closing his eyes, he leaned his head back against the pillow. His other hand caressed up his body until he was cupping his left pec, imagining that it was Klarissa's breast again. It was a dick that his hand was wrapped around, stroking, but he was trying to hold the image that his body was female and that she was fingering herself and rubbing her clit instead of the tip of the penis.

He couldn't hold onto that visualization like he used to be able to. But it still felt good, and he tried not to feel hypocritical for enjoying his currently male body. Once Calvin couldn't hold on to imagining himself as Klarissa, another figure entered his erotic fantasy. It was Machandi with a sea of stars behind her. She was nude and her figure was more beautiful than he could have anticipated. There was something sensuous about the contour of the blue alien's bald head. Her hips and breasts were full; more curvy than any woman that Calvin had ever been with. Calvin felt himself becoming even more aroused. Taking in her whole alluring form, he noticed that her nipples were dark blue as well as her pubic hair.

In this vision she smiled at him, her eyes sparkling like the stars behind her. Then she kneeled down and straddled him. He imagined the extraterrestrial taking his cock deep inside her. Machandi closed her eyes and tilted her head back, her earrings dangling on the sides of her neck. Calvin could almost feel her wet cunt around his cock as he squeezed it tighter with his hand. In the vision he put his hands on her ass as she rode him. Her glutes were perky and muscular like she worked out a lot. Calvin squeezed her ass and then caressed up her abs and over her voluptuous tits, noticing that her whole body was toned and muscular. Even her biceps were developed, and he touched them, the sexual exhilaration building from feeling her muscles.

"Oh my Goddess, I'm gonna cum," he said, moaning with the ecstasy building in his body. Putting his left hand under his testicles, Calvin began to press his fingers against his taint and massage it as he felt the orgasm building.

"I want you to cum inside me," the alien goddess said to him in his fantasy. "Cum! Give it to me!"

"Uhh God, oh fuck! I'm cumming!" Calvin screamed as his cock pulsed and the fluid rushed from his balls and up through his urethra. It gushed out with such force that it shot up his torso and he was shocked to feel it spray against his cheek. "Ohhhh..." He let out a huge sigh, feeling the tingles of the orgasm rushing through his body. With his eyes still closed, he could see Machandi smiling down at him and thought he felt her squeezing her pussy muscles around his cock as if she was trying to suck all of his semen into her.

The Pleiadian Goddess disappeared as he opened his eyes. As the afterglow continued to buzz through every tissue of his body, he wiped the cum off his cheek with his hand and then licked the rest off of his fingers and swallowed it. Calvin enjoyed the taste of himself. Both female secretion and male secretion were big turn-ons for him. There was definitely something sacred—something divine—about the fluids that came from the excitation of sexual energy.

Even though the erotic fantasy had ended, Calvin still found himself thinking about Machandi. Now that he wasn't in such an emotional state, he began thinking about what she had tried to convey to him when he was in the throes of full existential crisis. Granted, he wasn't feeling fully comfortable in his male body, as Calvin, but he was feeling a lot better than he had been. He wondered if it was only because it had been several days and he was getting used to being in this body again. Either way, he wasn't feeling the despair that he had been.

What seemed strange, when he thought about it, was that when she was Klarissa, she still retained all the memories of being Calvin. The same was true for when he was Calvin; he could recall all the memories of being Klarissa, even though he was operating as his male identity. Was the inner person—whatever that was—the same within both Calvin and Klarissa? He was trying to grasp this, but it wasn't quite becoming a full epiphany. There were still a lot of nuances that remained a mystery. Klarissa and Calvin were not completely separate people, that was abundantly clear since the other personality didn't black out when the other one took over; as in some cases of multiple personality or dissociative identity. But if they were the same person no matter what gender their body was, then how come they felt most comfortable and most like themself when they were in female form? He didn't quite have an answer for that yet.

Other than the fact that he was becoming insanely bored, Calvin figured Machandi was right and he needed to get a stack of books to read. That would pass the time when he didn't feel like practicing the yoga which seemed to not be getting him closer to controlling his Zeromorph. On top of that, it would help to get him out of his head and into some different perspectives which might help him get more of a handle on his own situation.

After throwing on some clothes, he fired up *The Quantum Shortbus* and headed into town. It was a beautiful Fall day and Calvin enjoyed the drive immensely. The leaves on the trees were turning colors and the Sun seemed to be smiling over the pleasant landscape of Mount Shasta. During the drive he almost forgot about his wish to be Klarissa again and was just enjoying life and the beauty of nature. Maybe the obsession with controlling the whole gendered experience was getting in the way of just enjoying the journey and where it was taking him. Was it really that important? Calvin still felt like it was, but he was questioning it more.

Pretty soon he was parking in front of *The Chai Shop*, wondering if it would be Atomsk or Lilith who would be there today. If it was Atomsk, he thought, would he recognize him as the same person he was with the other night? Calvin even contemplated pretending to be someone else; he wasn't ready to tell either one of them about being a Zeromorph. Looking at *The Chai Shop* out of his side window, he suddenly felt awkward about encountering Lilith or Atomsk. Logically he knew he shouldn't feel that way, they had all been intimate with each other and Calvin knew he should feel comfortable around them. He figured it probably had something to do with wanting to be Klarissa while his body was forcing him to be Calvin.

So he sucked it up and took a deep breath before going inside. When he came through the door, long blonde hair swinging, Lilith looked up from the book she was reading behind the counter. A big smile grew across her face at the sight of him. Calvin smiled back in a friendly way.

"Hey, Calvin!" she said, closing her book. "It's great to see you. I was wondering if you were going to show back up."

"It's good to see you too, Lilith," he offered back. His words were friendly but he did feel like he was more stand-offish than he normally would be. Why couldn't he jerk himself out of this funk? He pointed toward the little book area. "I came to, uh, check out what books you have."

"Oh, yeah, go ahead," Lilith said. "We've got a lot of stuff you wouldn't find anywhere else. Some cool and rare shit in there."

Calvin smiled and nodded. "Thanks," he said quickly and then rushed into the room with the books. There were so many choices it was almost overwhelming. He didn't really know where to start. What did he know about occult books?

Practically nothing. Even growing up he'd never been a big reader. He did remember liking fantasy stories and girly romance manga when he was in middle school and high school, but he was never a *heavy* reader. Not like these books that he was looking at now, running his finger along their spines and reading the obscure titles. Some of these volumes were *huge*. Calvin pulled out one hardcover book that contained all the teachings and rituals of the Hermetic Order of the Golden Dawn. It was a heavy tome; he flipped through the pages, shook his head, and then returned it to the shelf.

In an attempt to thwart the overwhelm of the task at hand, Calvin decided to try giving up the control his logical mind wanted to exert and instead trust his intuition and his Soulmind. When he did this, his hand was guided to pull five books from the shelves: *Sex and Rockets: The Occult World of Jack Parsons* by John Carter; *Musings on Human Metamorphoses* by Timothy Leary; *Sex, Drugs, & Magick* by Robert Anton Wilson; *Tantra: The Cult of the Feminine* by André van Lysebeth; and *Simulations of God* by John C Lilly. It felt right, it felt complete. These were the books that he was supposed to read. Calvin held this small stack of books in his hands and glanced at the covers and blurbs on the backs. These books were *weird*; definitely outside the scope of what he normally studied—if he even studied at all. They were almost outside his comfort zone. However, dealing with being a Zeromorph had been pushing him outside his comfort zone whether he wanted it or not. And his interactions with Atomsk and Lilith had definitely opened him up and taken him to places he hadn't imagined he'd go even in his wildest dreams.

Calvin took his little stack of books to Lilith at the front counter. "Just these," he said as he put the books down in front of the register and smiled even though he still felt off. It was a strain to pretend he was okay.

"Looks like you found some good stuff," she replied, picking up each book as she checked the prices. "Oh, especially this one by Robert Anton Wilson! I love it, I've read it a couple times."

"Thanks," Calvin said distractedly. "I hope I get something out of them. I've never read anything like this before."

"Oh, yeah?" Lilith asked. "Has something been on your mind? Deepening your journey into the Occult?"

"Something like that," he answered vaguely.

Lilith told him the total he owed for the books and he paid in cash. Then before Calvin could pick up his books and leave, she scooted out from behind the counter and approached him. He turned toward her just as she grabbed him by the waist and pulled his body into hers. She kissed him passionately on the lips and wrapped her arms around his back. After kissing his neck, she whispered in his ear, "I want you." Calvin pulled back a bit and when Lilith felt him pulling away she frowned and looked into his eyes. "Are you okay?" she asked. Her hands were around his waist again and his hands were on her shoulders.

"I'm just not feeling like myself right now," he responded. "I want you too, believe me. I just don't feel very well at the moment. I'm sorry."

She shrugged. "It's okay. I want you to take care of yourself, that's the most important thing," she said as she let go of Calvin and took a step away from him. "Self-love and self-care, I want those to be your highest priorities."

"Thanks," he said, picking up his books from the counter.

Lilith studied him for a moment, looking down at his body and then up at his face. "Are you eating okay?" she asked. "You look thin and when I touched you, you felt pretty skinny."

"I'm okay," Calvin replied hastily, anxious to leave.

"No," she shook her head and went back around to behind the counter. After getting out a paper bag, she put several vegan pastries and cookies in it from the display case. "I know it's not much," she continued, handing the bag to Calvin, "but take it. At least get some calories in you." She smiled as Calvin took the bag from her hand.

"Thanks a lot," he said. "I appreciate that."

"Take care of yourself, Calvin," Lilith called after him as he quickly walked to the door. "I'll see you soon."

Almost before he was done waving, he was out the door, Lilith watching him as he departed. Calvin opened the side door of the van and tossed the books in along with the bag of pastries. Being a Zeromorph was more complicated than he originally thought; it wasn't all just sex and orgasms. Yes, that was part of it, but there is more substance to a person than that. And being both man and woman, that meant dealing with the emotions and complexities of both. Calvin felt like he was wrestling with redefining what it meant to be masculine and what it meant to be feminine. *Come to think of it*, he thought, *what does it mean to be masculine—or feminine for that matter?*

As he drove back to the campsite, his mind was occupied with this conundrum. The stereotypes of men and women were well known, but each person was an individual. There were masculine women and feminine men and the whole spectrum in between. The key was to learn about himself—herself—themself—and what those characteristics meant uniquely to Calvin/Klarissa's own inner being. When he was Calvin, he found himself contemplating the nature of Klarissa. And when she was Klarissa, she had also contemplated the nature of Calvin. Could he break out of this feedback loop; or could he use it to learn more about himself—*herself*?

In the days that followed, Calvin felt like a monk on a solitary retreat into nature. A lot of this time he spent devouring the books he had bought at *The Chai Shop*. He couldn't remember the last time he had read so much; and it wasn't drudgery, he found the subject matter fascinating and relevant to his own situation. He felt like he was learning more than he had in a very long time. Long walks through the woods calmed him and he was beginning to feel more comfortable in Calvin's skin again since these few mornings hadn't brought Klarissa back.

During his walks through the lovely forest, Calvin would visualize *The Quantum Shortbus* as a spaceship, and mentally construct how he wanted the interior to look and how it would defy logic. He wanted the inside of his spaceship to be malleable and changeable, as fluid as his own imagination. The other fantasies that swam around his mind were ones of exploration, what planets and galaxies he would go see as he zoomed around the Spiralverse in *The Quantum Shortbus*. These thoughts would bring him joy, but he knew his magick wasn't that strong. He couldn't even get his body to change at will yet.

The yoga and meditation was still a constant practice. Obviously he knew that he was still far from mastery of these techniques. These esoteric methods had yet to yield results. Surprisingly, Calvin found himself getting less and less frustrated about not being able to control the Zeromorph. He wasn't exactly sure why this was and he was curious about it. However, his suspicion was that it most likely was an effect of the yoga and meditation. Even just in and of themselves those practices made him feel elevated, calm, and clear. This helped him to not feel like there was a sense of rush. Everything was slower out in nature, and Calvin enjoyed that.

There was a lot of information in those books—a lot of really beneficial information that Calvin could latch on to. But one specific concept that emerged for him, that he found especially lucrative to his own situation, was this concept of integration of opposites—and especially the integration of the feminine principle with the masculine principle. The book on Tantra stated that everyone had an inner masculine and feminine. Calvin hadn't really thought about this much before especially since society conditions people to believe that they are all one thing or the other. The revelation that *everyone* is male and female could be so liberating, he thought. The memory of the part in their LSD journey when they had held both male and female together was a little hazy, but Calvin remembered how right that had felt and how comfortable they had been as this Other Creature.

Calvin had always been more feminine, but ever since he had experienced that feminine nature externalized, he had wanted that at the expense of rejecting or fearing his more masculine side. Having this time to reflect and just be in his male body, he was learning more and more not to be so quick to reject that part of himself—Calvin was part of them after all. Calvin was just as much part of Klarissa as Klarissa was part of Calvin. And he was beginning to realize that. The opposites did not have to be mutually exclusive.

After a few days of this routine, it was early afternoon and Calvin had just finished reading a chapter in Robert Anton Wilson's *Sex, Drugs, & Magick*. He put the book down and decided to drop into a little meditation to see if he could excite the Zeromorph from its slumber. After coming into a cross-legged position on his bed, Calvin closed his eyes and rested his hands on his knees. He began some long deep breathing until his mind was tranquil like the undisturbed surface of a still pond. Then he began Breath of Fire, exciting his Kundalini, his Soulmind. After a few minutes of Breath of Fire, pumping his navel vigorously, Calvin took a deep breath and held it at the top. His eyes rolled up behind his eyelids and he focused at the center of his brow, the Third Eye, and he squeezed Root Lock, pushing his Kundalini to rise, illuminating the Soulmind as it traveled through each chakra. The yellow Soulmind energy spiraled at his heart chakra and called more energy up from the base of the spine. Yellow energy snaked up around the spine like the double helix of a DNA strand, connecting to the heart and then continuing its journey toward the crown. This yellow energy took its path through the throat, the Third Eye, and then exploded out of the Crown Chakra, igniting the aura around Calvin's head in a yellow glow like the rays of light when Buddha obtained enlightenment.

Calvin pushed all expectations out of his mind and felt an overwhelming sense of fulfillment. Whatever happened, he knew he was whole. Whatever he-she-it was, it was something essential and constant, an *essence* which was the heart. Nothing could ever take that away, no matter what the outside of the body looked like. "Trust. Love. Surrender," he whispered. He trusted the Zeromorph within to work with him and not against him, and in the innate wisdom of the the body, the cells. He loved his body, his physical form, whatever it looked like, whatever manifestation it chose to express. And finally he surrendered the need to control, the compulsion to exert his own will on a process that was natural and needed time to grow and evolve. As he felt more of his energy rising, the light making his head feel high, he was impelled to say something else. Taking a deep breath, he casted this spell: "Zero, do as you will. Zero, do as you will. Zero, do as you will..."

Then he exhaled all the air from his lungs, feeling the most deep relaxation as the tension he felt from the drive to be in command just melted away. He gave it up to the Spiralverse, or the Unified Field, or whatever that force has ever been called. And in that moment he felt the Zeromorph respond. There was a tingling in his pelvis and then he felt his body begin to change. His testicles and penis retracted toward his abdomen and melted into himself as if they were made of plasma. The testicles became ovaries and as his taint opened to produce the labia, the shaft of the penis pulled up and in creating the inside of the vagina and the clitoris. The chest grew a little as well, Klarissa's small breasts coming back into her thin figure.

Klarissa sat there, still in her yogic posture, almost not believing the Zeromorphosis had just taken place. Opening her eyes slowly, she checked herself, feeling her small breasts and then sliding her hand under the waistband of her sweatpants. No more male genitalia, the familiar feel of her vulva was there under her hand. Then she laughed, quietly at first and then her body shook with loud belly laughs. *Isn't it absurd*, she thought, *that I finally got the result once I gave up the desire and need to have it?*

# Ten

# Sex and Rocket Fuel

"**I**'m hungry," she said, feeling like the body of Klarissa hadn't eaten in a week. There might have been one can of soup left, but Calvin had eaten all the rest of the food. It was time to make a run to the grocery store. She threw on some more appropriate clothing and then fired up *The Quantum Shortbus.*

Klarissa enjoyed the drive as she sang along to whatever CD was playing. Without her even noticing, Machandi appeared in her plasma-body sitting in the front passenger's seat. "Looks like you got it to work," she said.

Klarissa jumped, surprised because she wasn't expecting to hear another voice. Turning her head to look at the blue goddess, she said, "Don't sneak up on me like that! Especially not when your girl is driving."

"You got your Zeromorph to change through surrender," Machandi continued.

"How'd you know that?" Klarissa asked.

"I might be watching even when you think I'm not," she replied, blue lips pulled into a smile.

"That's not creepy at all," Klarissa commented sarcastically.

"Surrender can be a good tool sometimes," Machandi elaborated. "The important thing is that you learn what you can from it. Let it dissolve your ego. But then you take back control right away."

"What do you mean?"

"You gave it up to a higher will and that higher will worked through you," the Pleiadian continued. "Remember that that higher will is just your own will on a different level. So bring it all back down under your will. The trick is to command the power but not to be attached to the outcome. Then the magick will really be under your control."

There was silence as Klarissa thought about this. Before she could think of something to say or a question to ask, Machandi was gone again, back out into the aether. *She's saying there's still a way to control the transformation,* she thought, *without letting the transformation control me.* But she didn't need to worry about that. She was who she wanted to be. *How long will it last this time?* she wondered. If her body tried to revert to male form too soon, Klarissa might have to attempt to exert her will over the Zero sooner than hoped for.

She didn't have to worry about that immediately, so she took her mind off of that inevitability and just enjoyed being Klarissa. Rolling her window down so she could feel the brisk mountain air, she considered her transformation to be a small victory. She might not have full mastery yet, but she was definitely one step closer to that condition. After the pleasant drive into town, Klarissa pulled into the parking lot of the local organic grocery store.

She only stocked up on foods that wouldn't go bad quickly and bought about enough to last her a week or two. As she was walking out with her bags, in that exact moment, Atomsk was walking up toward the entrance. He looked up and noticed her right away. "Klarissa," he said, his face brightening up.

"Hey, Atomsk," she said, returning the smile. Their paths had converged right next to *The Quantum Shortbus* and Klarissa was now opening the side door to load in the groceries. "How are you?"

"I'm good. How have you been?" Atomsk returned.

"I've been pretty good," she said.

"You still staying at that camp site near the mountain?"

"Yeah," Klarissa answered, putting the last two bags in the back of the van and closing the door. "Why?" she asked.

"No, I just," Atomsk started. "My brother lives on a junk-yard on the outskirts of town."

"Your brother lives in a junkyard?" she asked, raising her eyebrows.

"Well, it's his place," he answered. "He has a small house and lives there in his junkyard. He's an artist and inventor. Builds things out of the junk he collects."

"What kind of things?"

"Art. Machines," Atomsk continued. "I was thinking if you wanted a change of scenery you could park your van there for a while. He'd probably let you use his kitchen and keep some food in the refrigerator."

Klarissa hesitated. She'd been getting used to her little fairy spot in the middle of the forest. "But I like the forest," she said.

"If you're worried about him hitting on you," he went on, "don't be. Cause he's gay."

"A gay guy who lives in a junkyard and makes art?" she laughed. "That's not something you hear everyday."

Klarissa ended up following Atomsk as he led the way in his Subaru Outback. *They must go camping a lot too*, she thought. This brother's junkyard was on the outskirts of town, but on the opposite side of where she had been camping. As they finally approached the place, she could see it now on their right hand side. It was a big open field strewn with scrapped cars and other rusted machines in various states of disrepair. In the center of this twisted metal labyrinth was this guy's house. It was small, like a ranch house, and had only one floor. As both Klarissa and Atomsk parked their vehicles on the gravel in front of this house, a guy came out to greet them.

This man looked to be in his mid-thirties. His jet-black hair was slicked back with gel and looked almost vampiric. He was thin and wore a nice navy blue sweater with a pair of khakis. As they got out of their cars, Atomsk went to go greet his brother. "Do what thou wilt shall be the whole of the law," the brother said by way of greeting.

"Love is the law. Love under will," Atomsk replied. They smiled widely at each other and embraced. Then they turned to Klarissa. "This is my brother Buck."

"Nice to meet you," Buck said, extending his hand.

"You as well," Klarissa replied, shaking his hand.

"Hey, you two want to see my new piece of art?" Buck asked, almost conspiratorially.

"Fuck yeah I want to see some *art*," she said excitedly.

Buck motioned for them to follow him and he circled around to the back of the house. There, amid piles of metal scraps, was a miniature rocket ship made out of car parts that had once seen better days. This rocket was about as tall as a person and Klarissa went to inspect it. It was sort of a Frankenstein-looking machine. Each panel was a different color because each came from a different car. There was a dome window near the top of the rocket. Klarissa wondered where Buck had come across that part. The rocket also had three fins that jutted down around its thrusters. "This one obviously is purely sculpture," Buck explained. "It won't be making it to the Moon anytime soon. However, I am experimenting with making rocket fuel."

"Have you heard of Jack Parsons?" Klarissa asked.

"Of course," Buck said. "I study a lot of his work when it comes to rockets and the occult."

"I just read *Sex and Rockets*," she continued. "Do you know that book about Jack Parsons?"

"I read that one," he answered. "Enjoyed it a lot. I have a suspicion though that they might not have been totally accurate about the details of the Babalon Working."

"I was wondering that too," Klarissa admitted. "Still found the whole thing so fascinating. Especially his connection with the Scientology guy."

"L. Ron Hubbard," Atomsk interjected.

"Right," she said, remembering. "Hey, Buck," she continued, "do you think you could make my van into a rocket ship?"

"That's a weird question," he commented. "But, yeah, I think I could do it."

"Atomsk, what does it mean to be a man?" Klarissa asked later as she and Atomsk were taking a walk through the maze of junk.

"That's a loaded question," he responded. "I think that's something that we give just as much meaning to as we want it to have. To one person it could be meaningful and to another person equally meaningless. But don't get me wrong, there are legitimate and tangible qualities to both the divine feminine and divine masculine."

"For example?"

"The masculine needs to know how to hold space so the feminine can blossom," he continued. "The masculine should know how to provide that safety and extend a sense of security towards the feminine. And the feminine is more receptive and creative."

"Y'know, Timothy Leary said that we're all evolving into space beings," Klarissa interjected. "I wonder if when we're at that point if we'll have transcended the duality of genders. Maybe we'll all be androgynous hermaphrodites who travel for fun through time and space. We'll be able to have sex with all different types of genders and alien species. There will be no need for silly gender roles when we're all advanced gods with no fixed orientation or sex."

"Is that how you envision the future?" Atomsk asked.

"Well, yeah..." she admitted. "Why? How do you see the future?"

"I don't know," he shrugged. "I haven't really thought about it. I'm more of a live-in-the-moment type of person."

"How are you ever supposed to shape your future when you can't see past what's right in front of you?" Klarissa asked. She stopped walking and turned to look at Atomsk.

He returned her look with a suggestive smile. "You want to see how I shape my future?" And before she could respond, Atomsk had her by the waist and pulled her into him. He pressed his lips against hers and she returned his kiss. While they were making out, Klarissa began fumbling with his belt. She could feel the bulge of his erection pressing against the front of his jeans. Finally getting the belt undone, she pulled his pants down as she dropped to her knees. Atomsk's cock was semi-hard and directly at the level of Klarissa's face. Without a pause she took his dick into her mouth and began to suck and lick it as she massaged his balls with her right hand.

Klarissa's other hand was down her pants and rubbing her swollen clit. She moaned as Atomsk got fully hard and she could feel the tip of his dick at the back of her throat. His dick twitched and Klarissa almost thought he was going to cum in her mouth. But then he put his hands around the sides of her face and pulled her back up towards him until they were kissing again. Now she was fumbling with her own pants. Quickly they were off and kicked aside on the dusty ground. She was wet and could feel her own lubrication dripping down the inside of her thigh.

Atomsk's arms were so muscular and he could easily pick all one hundred and ten pounds of her up off the ground. Wrapping his large hands around her ass cheeks, he pulled her up and towards him. Klarissa's feet flew off the ground and she regained her balance again with the bottoms of her feet against the front of his thighs. Then he guided her pelvis down onto his dick. Her arms were around his neck, keeping most of her weight on his shoulders. It wasn't exactly weightless lovemaking, but it was some sort of acrobatic sex. She bounced up and down on his shaft, her eyes closed and mouth slightly open as she moaned. How Atomsk had lasted like this without busting a nut inside her was beyond Klarissa's imagination. She could even feel her cunt getting close to orgasm.

"Oh my God, that feels so fucking good," she moaned. "Keep going like that and you're gonna make me cum."

"Give me a warning," Atomsk said. "I want to drink it when you squirt."

"I feel the energy growing in my cunt... Fuck, I'm so wet," she said breathily. "Oh shit!" she shrieked suddenly. "I'm gonna cum! I'm gonna cum!"

He lifted her off of his cock as easily as if she had been a doll and set her down so her feet were on the ground again. Wasting no time, he dropped to his knees and opened his mouth so he could catch every drop of whatever dripped out of her snatch. Klarissa worked her clit until she felt the orgasm explode, traveling from her clitoris to her spine and up to her brain.

"Give it to me," Atomsk said, his eager tongue out and salivating.

"Oh fuck! Ooooooooohhh God yes!" she came in that moment, her pelvic muscles spasming with the ecstasy, squirting into his awaiting mouth. He swallowed every drop of it and licked his lips as Klarissa sprayed him one last gush across the face. She looked down at Atomsk between her legs. He smiled at her and she began to laugh, caught off guard by the look of his face covered in her cum. "I feel like that wasn't the first time I've given you a facial."

"You're welcome to sit on my face anytime you like," he said as he stood up and wiped his face with his shirt. Klarissa was already putting her pants back on and Atomsk followed suit. It was easy for him since he only needed to pull his pants up and buckle his belt. He hadn't taken his pants and shoes completely off during their fuck sesh. They were in a junkyard, after all. There was never telling what kind of sharp objects or hazards might be around. Klarissa was obviously the more adventurous one, even sitting down on the gravel of the junkyard ground barefoot before slipping her shoes back on.

"You know you'd love to go down there and sniff my asshole," she said, raising her eyebrows.

"I might have thought about it," Atomsk admitted. "And if it was right after a shower I might even eat your asshole too."

"That sounds hot," Klarissa responded. She hit him playfully in the chest. "Don't get me all horny again. That's not fair." Smiling up at Atomsk, she gave him puppy-dog eyes. He leaned down and kissed her on the lips before they started walking back toward Buck's house. "Atomsk, I've been reading about this idea of integrating opposites. Balancing both masculine and feminine."

"You mean the Divine Androgyne?" he said. "In Tantra it's the Shiva and the Shakti. In the Tao it's the Yin and Yang."

"Do you feel like you've integrated your feminine side and masculine side?" she asked.

Atomsk nodded. "Yeah, I think I have. Either way I have Lilith to balance me out—and you. However, you seem to be something else entirely. Something a lot more chaotic."

"I feel like that's me," Klarissa said, as if having the realization for the first time. "I am the Divine Androgyne and I am both man and woman."

"You do seem to have this very sexually ambiguous energy about you sometimes," he commented. "Actually the balancing of the female principle with the male principle usually refers to a man and a woman having sex and returning to that androgynous state where they melt into each other. This is key in Sex Magick. Crowley called it *The Beast with Two Backs*."

"For me I experience it more as an internal process," Klarissa explained. "Like my own bi-sexual soul is the laboratory for Alchemical synthesis. I no longer feel the split between my male part and my female part."

"But you are a woman," he interjected. "I'm pretty sure I was just inside you."

"Don't fall into the trap of thinking that gender is only skin deep," she replied as she grabbed his crotch and squeezed. "Your dick and balls here don't make you a man."

"I know," he said quickly. "We're all androgynous. I have an inner Shakti just as you have an inner Shiva."

"I'm something beyond all that," Klarissa said in a dreamy voice as she stared out over the piles of junk. "I want to go by Timothy Leary's pronouns. Since we are evolving into space beings."

"The ones he used to specify gender neutrality?" Atomsk returned.

"I like them," she informed. "S/he with a slash between the 'S' and the 'H.' And hir with an 'i.' I feel more comfortable being referred to by those, and for some reason to me they have a sort of futuristic vibe to them. Sometimes I just want to fuck with people though when they ask 'what are your pronouns' by giving them the answer 'he-she-it.' Always wondered if someone might refer to me as 'it.'"

"You'd be the biggest 'It' to me, with a capital I, if you turned out to be an alien," he said jokingly, giving her a wink.

"Do you ever wonder if we're just God simulating herself so we can experience that Self?" Klarissa asked, totally seriously.

"All the time," Atomsk answered, equally as serious.

Then they both burst out laughing.

Buck had a guest bedroom in his little house, so Klarissa naturally claimed that while he took *The Quantum Shortbus* into the Laboratory, which is what he called the barn. He used that space for welding and sculpting mostly. A couple days later she went to get a book out of the back of her van. She had finished reading all the other books. *Simulations of God* was the only book she hadn't finished yet. Upon going into the barn, Klarissa could see all the hard work Buck was putting in to transform *The Quantum Shortbus*. Two thrusters had already been attached to the back door of the van. She wondered where he had found those parts, or if he welded them together from panels of other things. Buck had a face shield protecting him while he used a blowtorch on the underside of the second thruster.

"It looks good!" Klarissa commented. "Next thing you're going to tell me is that it can go back in time too."

Buck laughed. "That would be cool, wouldn't it?" he said. "If we could travel through time, where would you want to go?"

"I'd want to go to the future," she said.

"Huh," he started. "Most people would want to go to some romanticized notion of the past. To relive some golden age. Maybe Paris in the '20s. But you—you want to go see the future. I like that."

"I just wanted to come grab this book I was reading," Klarissa explained as she popped open the van's side door and fished out the book.

"What is it?" Buck asked.

She showed him the cover of the book. "*Simulations of God* by John C Lilly," she read.

"John C Lilly," he repeated. "I've read *The Center of the Cyclone* but not this one."

"These books will blow your mind like a good hit of some LSD," Klarissa continued. "Buck, do you think I'll ever reach space in this thing?"

"There are only limits if you choose to put those limits on your imagination," he answered. "Now, I have switched your spaceship to run on solid fuel. Did the Wright Brothers know their invention would get off the ground before they did it? Probably not. But do I know *The Quantum Shortbus* will carry you into adventures you can't even as of yet fathom? Yes! You know why? Because every man and every woman is a Star."

Klarissa woke up at midnight in a haze. She had smoked a lot of weed before going to bed and still felt pretty high. All she wore was a pair of gray sweatpants and a baggy hoodie as she left the guest room. Buck's soft snoring could be heard as she walked by the closed door of his bedroom. It was as if Klarissa was in a daze, almost being led in a trance out toward her spaceship. Her brain was like a computer wiping itself of outdated software to make room for more advanced programs. The idea of God making a simulation to inhabit and experience just so that It could make a bigger simulation of Itself but would only be able to experience it through the level of the human simulation.

There was a silver full moon hanging high over the junkyard and was almost so bright that it illuminated the whole property. The other thing that Klarissa noticed was how foggy it was. There was a heavy mist hanging in the air, giving the junkyard an eerie feeling. She pushed her way through a side door on the barn and closed it behind her. There was *The Quantum Shortbus* in all its glory. All three thrusters were attached to the back and it looked like it was ready to zoom around the Spiralverse.

Klarissa crawled in through the side door and got into lotus pose on the fold-down bed. Closing her eyes, she assumed the yogic breathing—slow, long, and deep. She didn't even have to do Breath of Fire to excite the Kundalini this time. Her yellow Soulmind ignited at the root chakra and the heart chakra. Then the golden snakes traveled up the spine in a spiral, like DNA strands. It was like a rocket that shot up from her pelvic floor and burst in the pineal gland. In the inner vision, when the Soulmind hit the center of the brain, Klarissa's physical body became no more and all she was was golden light energy. She could feel that she possessed something like a plasma-body that resembled an ethereal yellow ghost. Then, spinning within the tendrils of yellow Soulmind consciousness, a huge DNA strand began to take shape. As if possessed by intuition or instinct,

Klarissa took her plasma arms consisting of pure consciousness and began to dismantle and disassemble the big yellow DNA strand.

Even though she didn't know what she was doing, Klarissa didn't stop. She broke that DNA down into pieces, and then like a metaphysical architect, began to build it back up again. All she knew was that what *she* was creating was the real s/he. Hir real face and hir real body. Then a name was spoken in hir own voice: "Ckaspian!" The name was also written out in hir imagination with the wisps of yellow energy.

Speaking the name out loud became the catalyst for the transformation. S/he felt hir yellow energy body assimilate with the physical body once more. And as the new configuration of DNA rendered in hir body, Ckaspian could feel something growing out above hir clitoris. Hir small breasts remained the same, or maybe shrank a little. And that was it—that Zeromorphosis wasn't too dramatic. Just growing a dick over the vagina—no balls—and the breasts. Ckaspian felt the androgyne gender lock in place and s/he knew that s/he had integrated the opposites. To hold two contradictorics at once is a paradox—and s/he was one; the next stage of evolution. In spite of the excitement of gaining that much more mastery over the Zero, all Ckaspian could think about was showing Atomsk.

Right when s/he had that thought, the sound of a car driving up could be heard. S/he guessed that it was Atomsk because who else would be out at the junkyard at this time of night? Ckaspian's yellow aura buzzed as s/he shook hir head out of the trance. With a smile on hir face, s/he climbed out of *The Quantum Shortbus* and out of the barn to greet hir lover. At the same moment that Ckaspian was approaching the parked Subaru Outback, fog shimmering in its headlights, the front door of the small house flapped open and out ran Atomsk.

Ckaspian stopped and stared, because s/he had been expecting him to get out of the car and not out of the front door of the house. As if in slow motion, the driver's side door of the Subaru opened and out stepped Lilith into the fog. She stared with an expression of disbelief from Atomsk to Ckaspian, obviously not expecting to see these two together. Finally, she just stared at Ckaspian and crossed her arms, her mouth hanging open in astonishment. Then Lilith's question was just one word: "Calvin?"

# Eleven

## Elysian Secretions

"Wait, what?" Atomsk said, staring at Ckaspian in the mist and then back at his wife. "Klarissa, why did she just call you Calvin?"

"So *this* is what you've been doing out here all this time?" Lilith continued. "Honestly, I almost thought you were out here fucking your brother."

"I'm not—that...gay," he tried to seem offended, starting off strong and then ending weak.

"I can see that," she commented, giving Ckaspian a look. "Or maybe I don't see. This is *who* now? Calvin, can you explain this to me?"

"We said we were opening up our marriage," Atomsk interjected.

Lilith furrowed her eyebrows and shot an angry look at her husband while she pointed her finger at him. "No, *you* said we were opening up our marriage."

"Well, if you *know* this Calvin the way I know Klarissa, then you have no room to judge me!" he retorted and then went silent for a minute, trying to think about the meaning of what he just said.

Ckaspian didn't know what to say. They both thought they knew hir, but they only knew the half. "Wait," Lilith started, looking hard at Ckaspian now. "You mean we're both fucking the same guy?"

"She didn't have a penis when I fucked her!" Atomsk exclaimed, getting more confused by the second. Then he looked at Ckaspian. "I gather by now that you've also fucked my wife. Klarissa, how do you know her more than just from visiting *The Chai Shop*?"

Lilith approached Ckaspian with her arms crossed. Atomsk was already closer to the androgyne, studying hir in the dark light of the night. He could tell something was different about hir, but he couldn't place what it was; the familiarity of Klarissa was still enough there to make him question. And Lilith thought she was talking to Calvin, but now she wasn't so sure. "Yeah, Calvin—or Klarissa," Lilith said almost in a whisper. "Why don't you explain to us who the fuck you are, since it seems like we've both already fucked you."

"I'm a Zeromorph," Ckaspian explained, finally getting a word in. "I wanted to tell you guys. I was going to tell your husband but I couldn't figure out how to say it."

"You're what? A shapeshifter?" Lilith asked.

"Sort of," Ckaspian went on. "I can transform back and forth between male and female. I wasn't able to control it so well at first. So sometimes I was Klarissa or Calvin when I didn't want to be. But I just had another transformation and I think I'm getting control of the Zero."

"So who are you *now*?" Atomsk asked. "You look like Klarissa."

"And you look like Calvin," Lilith added.

"I've assimilated them both," Ckaspian continued. "So now I'm both of them in one, which makes me something else. You can call me Ckaspian. And refer to me by Timothy Leary's pronouns: hir and s/he with a slash."

Lilith laughed. "That's bullshit. This sounds like bullshit to me. Caspian like from Narnia?"

"I spell it with a 'K' after the 'C.'"

"Well, that explains it then!" Atomsk said sarcastically. "The 'K' explains it all! Prove it. Prove that you're this Zero-shifter."

"Okay," Ckaspian said as s/he opened hir pants and pulled them down.

There was definitely a penis there between hir legs and Atomsk couldn't fathom it. "How the fuck did you do that?" he asked. Ckaspian winked at him and put hir finger up to her lips as s/he pulled up hir penis in order to show the vulva underneath it. "What the fuck?" he said, not knowing how to process what he was seeing. "I've never seen anything like *that* before." He stood up and turned around, putting his hands over his face.

"I knew you were a fucking alien," Lilith said with a smile as she walked back over to her car.

"I'm not a fucking alien!" Ckaspian said, exasperated. "I might be evolving into a space being, but I am still a human who happens to be a Zeromorph. There's nothing extraterrestrial about it... Or, well, there might be." S/he pulled hir pants back up and followed Lilith around to the back passenger door of the Subaru Outback.

"You know, I really thought about you after that time you came in and bought all those books," she said, turning to face Ckaspian. "I was definitely getting this spacey vibe from you. I knew you'd be okay. That's what you meant when you said you weren't feeling like yourself. I couldn't have imagined the reality of your transformation. But yeah, my intuition guided me to another book that might benefit you on your quest. I kept the book in the car in case I saw you around town and could give it to you. But I guess *this* is why I haven't seen you." She motioned with her head to indicate the junkyard.

After opening the car door, Lilith picked up the book off the seat and handed it to Ckaspian. "*God Games* by Neil Freer," s/he said, reading the cover of the paperback. "How did you know?"

"How did I know what?" Lilith replied.

"About the book?" Ckaspian elaborated. "About how I want to play god games in different galaxies, and how did you know about the spaceship?"

"It was just the vibe I got from you," she said, shrugging. "I don't know anything about any spaceship."

"That's my wish," Ckaspian explained, "to have adventures in space. And fuck all the aliens throughout all star systems."

Lilith laughed. "You are definitely a Futant if I've ever met one."

"What's a Futant?" s/he asked.

"That's another Leary-ism," she continued, staring off through the fog toward her husband who was walking back to the car. "It's a combination of Future and Mutant. You're definitely a mutant and that might be our path to the future. That's the question we have to figure out about our marriage, me and Atomsk. Are we going to evolve or are we going to go extinct?"

Ckaspian didn't say anything. S/he liked both of them—s/he maybe even *loved* them. But s/he didn't want to become the reason a marriage broke apart. There could always be other ways; different paths to take toward a more evolved future. How could they choose to grow instead of dismantle?

"I'm sorry," Atomsk said to his wife from the other side of the car. "I know I should have told you."

"And I could have told you too but I didn't," Lilith said gratingly. "Now get in the car, babe. We have some stuff we need to talk about."

"Is it me?" Ckaspian asked, concerned. "I don't want to drive you two away."

"It's not you. Well—some of it is. Anyway, we'll be back later," she assured hir. "Love you," Lilith said and kissed Ckaspian lightly on the lips. She got in the passenger's side and

Atomsk got in the driver's seat. Ckaspian stared into the heavy mist as hir two lovers drove off out of the junkyard. Carrying hir book, s/he pouted as s/he went back into the barn to be around hir beloved *Quantum Shortbus*. *The confrontation had been inevitable*, s/he told hirself. Could there have been a better way of breaking the news that both husband and wife were cheating on each other with the same person? It was the secrecy that really needed to be done away with. Couldn't they all be free to love each other openly? Okay, there was blame on all sides. Ckaspian had failed to divulge the truth of hir identity to either of hir sexual partners. And the husband and wife failed to divulge to each other that they were seeing someone else sexually. So there was deception all around. But Ckaspian wanted to go beyond all those petty monogamous human sexual norms. Could the three of them together make sense?

As Ckaspian sat on the fold-down bed in the back of the van, s/he flipped through the pages of the new book Lilith had given hir. Using intuition, s/he let hir finger be guided to a passage that stuck out at hir like a magick spell. After pulling out a pen and notepad from a bin under the bed, she copied down the passage from the book and then hung it up on the wall. S/he read this passage by Neil Freer aloud and used it to cast a spell:

*"'I demand from the universe the greatest degree of freedom of which I can conceive. I demand that the universe teach me about even greater degrees of freedom than I can currently conceive. I demand answers from the universe that will satisfy my capacity to understand anything that I wish to know. I demand the fullest de-*

*gree of pleasure and happiness of which I am capable. I demand the freedom to demand. I demand the ability to play any game that I can conceive of an intelligence...playing at the 'level' of creating universes, interacting with other intelligences of the same or other kinds at that level in whatever modes of interaction I prefer or wish to create.'"*

Ckaspian felt like s/he could feel *The Quantum Shortbus* rumble with anticipation. The transformation to spaceship was almost complete and its desire to get into space was tactile. Buck's magick senses must have been tingling because he woke up and knew there were occult forces at work. All these energies were centered around Ckaspian and the spaceship. Before he even knew where he was, Buck came walking through the door of the barn wearing his red plaid pajamas.

The van's side doors were wide open so Buck could see Ckaspian inside sitting on the bed. "How does she look?" he asked. "Do you like what I did with these modifications?"

He meant the back thrusters and the way the engines interacted with the solid fuel. "I love it," Ckaspian said. "I can tell she's just itchin' to get off the ground. So much so I was just casting a spell to invoke playing at a higher level of creation."

"The frequency of this machine is very high," Buck continued. "But I think the whole molecular makeup needs to be transformed magickally before it can take you as far as you need to go."

"Some powerful Sex Magick," s/he responded. "I've been thinking that too. Especially to transform the inside here."

S/he looked around at the shabby inside of the van, strewn with hir belongings, food, and clothes. "If this is going to be a proper spaceship, worthy of an androgynous space being like myself, then I need to have a giant interior that shapes itself according to my imagination."

"You're going to need a powerful spell for that," Buck surmised. "And a fuck lot of energy."

"It could work," Ckaspian said with a sly smile. "We could build up that much energy. If I could get Lilith and Atomsk and you into a magickal foursome fuck-fest. I mean—you fuck your brother anyway."

"I *don't* fuck my brother!" Buck said indignantly. "It was all strictly magickal, I tell you. Just hands, ritual masturbation and stuff to cast spells. We never used mouths or penetration."

"Okay, I can work with that," the androgynous space being proclaimed. "And I don't think it would be that hard for me to get either of them on board. I did seduce both of them, after all. Or did they seduce me?"

"It kind of fucks with the mind a little bit, don't it?" Buck stated rhetorically. "That seems to be the way with these sexual relationships. You wonder who seduced who and how you found yourself balls deep in a stranger's asshole. Do you know what I mean?"

"I don't know..." Ckaspian started. "Maybe I do. This thing with Atomsk and Lilith seems like it happened much by accident. But sometimes I wonder if it was destined. Maybe I'm the catalyst that was needed in their relationship as well."

Suddenly they heard a car drive up near the outside of the barn and park. Before Ckaspian could even step out of the van, Lilith and Atomsk were in the barn, coming at hir from both sides somehow. "We both want you," Lilith said. Buck just stood there, largely ignored in that moment. "We both want you to be with us." She gestured to her husband and then back to herself. "Basically I was upset because I felt like Atomsk was keeping you here all to himself. I was jealous. I wanted time with you too. We have a strong dyad, me and him. But with you, I think we'll be an even stronger triad."

"Yes, I want to be with you both," Ckaspian said, putting an arm around each of their shoulders. Then s/he kissed Lilith and then Atomsk. "I'm glad we can open up this relationship to the three of us."

"We're just whores for *you*, no matter what you are... But I have to punish Atomsk," Lilith said, looking evilly at her husband. "You kept Klarissa here all to yourself and you didn't share her with me? I might have wanted some of that sweet moonflower too." She smacked him on top of the head playfully. "Evolve or die. Monogamy is dead and space is the new frontier, baby. Or is that what they say?"

"I have to be punished?" Atomsk asked, shocked. "I didn't really do anything that you didn't do too."

"I totally thought you were boning your brother," Lilith said offhand, looking over at Buck as if to include him in the conversation.

"It was strictly magickal," Buck said defensively. "Just ritual masturbation."

"Oh, yeah?" she said wickedly. "But you wanted to. Now you gotta suck his dick."

"What? That's fucked up," Atomsk said. "Why would you want to see me suck my brother's dick?"

Lilith shrugged. "Cause I'm a pervert. Do you need any other reason than that?"

"You are a filthy pervert," her husband shot back as he walked over in front of his brother and put his hands on his shoulders.

"Oh, I don't need a speech before you do it," Buck said, feeling like his brother was about to say something about 'breaking taboos' or some such. "And don't you try to make out with me."

Atomsk dropped to his knees and pulled his brother's pajama pants down. He swallowed hard and then put that cock in his mouth. Lilith had the biggest smile on her face as she watched the brother-on-brother oral incest. "Look, look," she poked Ckaspian with her elbow and indicated for hir to watch as Atomsk deep-throated his brother. "Even though he didn't say it," Lilith continued in a whisper, "breaking of the taboo does create an immensely larger amount of energy. That's why family members would often perform Sex Magick together so as to get that added boost of energy."

"Why does it create more energy?" Ckaspian wondered.

"Because it's releasing something sexually that society tells us to suppress," Lilith explained. "Acting out that forbidden deed releases that type of energy. Perfect for utilizing with magick. Watch them."

Atomsk had grabbed Buck's ass cheeks and squeezed his glutes as he pulled his brother's hips, guiding his cock deep into his throat. As he worshipped that dick, Atomsk had his head tilted up, his eyes closed, and his face flush as he sucked and licked that erection. "Oh my God, bro!" Buck shivered. "Suck that cock. Play with my balls."

Lilith felt wicked as her hand found its way into her pants. She played with her clit and slid two fingers into her wet cunt. Her husband's left hand played with his brother's testicles and his right hand found its way around to fondle his asshole. Then Lilith couldn't contain herself anymore and she raced over to stand next to Buck so she could look down at her husband as his head bobbed on his brother's cock. She pulled her pants down, exposing her dripping pussy. "Come lick my fucking cunt, Ckaspian," she commanded, "if you're such the Cosmic Slut that you say you are."

A proposition didn't have to be put in front of Ckaspian more than once before s/he was on that with whatever genitalia was called for. Right now what was needed was hir tongue deep inside Lilith. S/he found hirself there, kneeling next to Atomsk as he serviced Buck, giving great head to the wife of this man who had a dick in his mouth. "Fuck me, that's so hot," Lilith said, looking down at her husband licking the dick. She reached her hand out and ran her fingers through his hair. "Suck that fucking cock," she said, and moaned, getting herself all turned on. Then she looked down at Ckaspian. "Keep licking just like that. Uhhh, God..." Now Lilith was gripping Ckaspian's hair and grinding hir face right into her clitoris. "Oh, Ckaspian, make me cum!"

she shrieked. Then she came, her pelvis shaking against Ck-aspian's face and mouth. Hir face was wet with Lilith's juices when s/he pulled hir face away from the woman's crotch. As s/he gasped for air, she wiped the female jiz from hir cheeks.

"We should all go fuck in *The Quantum Shortbus*," Ck-aspian said. "It wants all our energy to transform it. We can create the magick!"

Atomsk's aura was even visible now, blazing blue around him. Buck's aura was green and flickered against his skin. The two energies played with each other and would some-times dance, weaving the two colors together in a surreal wash of fire. "Who the fuck are you even right now?" Lilith asked, pulling Ckaspian's face up to look in her eyes. "You're like some ethereal space being that just made me cum. I see Calvin in there, but there's more than Calvin."

"That's because I'm Ckaspian and this is my spaceship," s/he said excitedly, running up and flopping hirself down on the bed inside *The Quantum Shortbus*. "Welcome to my ves-sel," s/he said as s/he commenced to strip off all hir clothes and toss them on the floor. S/he looked so much like a delicate fairy sitting there—skin so pale and hair long and blonde. Hir shape was feminine and thin, with small hints of breasts. If it weren't for the penis-without-testicles, s/he looked to be all woman. Lilith didn't waste any time kicking off her pants and then losing her shirt. Naked, she pounced on Ckaspian, kissing hir face and neck as she stroked the shaft and fingered hir at the same time.

As Lilith was pleasuring Ckaspian, Buck sat on the floor of the van and got naked himself. Atomsk was also laying beside Ckaspian before s/he even realized he had taken his clothes off. The sexual energy was heightening exponentially, squared by each individual present and sharing their erotic power. Moving down hir torso, Lilith kissed Ckaspian's breasts and belly. Then she took hir cock in her mouth as she continued to finger-fuck the pussy underneath. As Ckaspian began to moan, Atomsk found hir mouth with his mouth. They kissed passionately as their tongues curled around each other's, longing for each other as their faces got wet with the mixture of their salivas. As Lilith continued to work her mouth between hir legs, it excited her aura, bringing out its flames of red.

As he continued to kiss Ckaspian, Atomsk stroked his cock, turned on by hir tongue and the sight of his wife going down on hir. After another couple minutes of bathing in the bliss of their four-way share of energy, Ckaspian pulled Lilith's head up off of hir cock, looked at them both, and said, "I want to feel you both. We should all be one. The three becomes one in a triune force."

Buck continued to stroke himself as he watched the three of them play. Ckaspian got up on hir knees with hir ass toward Atomsk. Lilith was up on her knees too as s/he guided her toward hir androgynous cock. Atomsk knew what to do. He pressed his body up against hir from behind, his cock held against hir supple ass. Ckaspian purred in a lustful way as s/he pushed her hips back onto his erection. His hands found their way to cupping hir breasts as he guided himself into hir from behind. "Uhh, yeah," s/he moaned as s/he looked over hir shoulder and kissed Atomsk on the lips. He thrusted a couple times deep into hir.

Lilith came closer from in front of Ckaspian, hir hands guiding her hips toward hir awaiting cock. Then s/he was inside her, Lilith gasping with orgasmic sighs. Ckaspian was euphoric; s/he could feel the fullness of being filled by Atomsk but also the penetration of being inside Lilith. "Well, anyone who has sex with me is instantly bisexual," Ckaspian quipped.

All four of them laughed, but didn't stop their sexual momentum. "This is the sexiest thing I've ever seen," Buck said breathily as he jerked himself off, his cock throbbing with the pressure of a coming orgasm.

"Don't cum yet," Ckaspian breathed, s/he was swaying in a sexual trance between her two Tantric partners on either side of hir. The couple seemed like they were devouring hir, kissing and sucking on hir neck and chest. "Save that cum for when we cum," s/he continued. "Then we'll use your energy to triple the magick. Ohh, god, fuck me..."

Atomsk thrusted into hir from the back, hands on hir hips as he slid his whole length and girth into hir while his wife rode this hermaphrodite's cock on the other side. "I fucking love you both," he gushed out as he felt the auras of all three of them braiding together. His blue energy snaked through Ckaspian's yellow energy which laced through Lilith's red energy.

As the edges of their individualities became more blurry, Ckaspian felt like s/he could tap into the pleasure and experience of her two partners. Sending hir inner Calvin out in energy form could let him latch on to the energy-body of Atomsk. Same with the energy form of Klarissa attaching itself to Lilith. And all at once Ckaspian didn't feel like hirself anymore, s/he felt like hir hermaphrodite had split and s/he was inside each half of the dyad which was Lilith and Atomsk torn apart. It was like s/he was fucking hirself from both sides, trying to merge all of their parts back together. Then s/he was suddenly back in the center, as Ckaspian, feeling every sensation as hir lovers thrust against hir sweating body between them.

"And I love it when you're both inside of me," the space being pronounced mystically. "When it feels like both of you are melting into the integration of both my Calvin and my Klarissa. The three of us becoming genderless. A triple-genital connection that is cosmically vast."

"I don't think I can hold back the explosion when you talk like that," Lilith said, kissing Ckaspian's mouth hungrily while Atomsk kissed and sucked the side of hir cheek. "I'm gonna cum all over your dick."

"I know it's about to explode so focus on building the inside of this spaceship," Ckaspian gasped out, holding hir orgasm back. "Train your energy to enhance mine as I create this interior space."

"Okay, I'm gonna cum," Atomsk said, his words quivering. "This is turning me on too much and I can't hold back."

"Cum with me!" Ckaspian screamed. "All of you cum with me!"

In that moment her cunt and her cock exploded with the wettest and most intense orgasm ever felt this side of the

Spiralverse. It shook the whole barn as Atomsk ejaculated inside of Ckaspian at the same time his wife lost control of her pussy muscles and spasmed an orgasm as she squirted lube all over their sandwiched lover's cock.

Then as Buck orgasmed too, jiz spraying far out of the tip of his cock, Ckaspian latched onto that energy with hir Soulmind, pulling their combined orgasm power into a point within hir Third Eye. It illuminated four sparks, one for each color of their Soulminds, which were all fully activated in that moment. Then s/he psychically sent those sparks down to hir heart chakra and exploded them outward, sending the spell to transform *The Quantum Shortbus* with all of their sexual energy backing it up.

As Ckaspian began to envision the inside of the spaceship with hir eyes closed, the interior began to change in real life. They almost thought they were hallucinating as they watched the inside of the van disappear and become a large white circular room with one main window over what looked like a long command console. There were two white futuristic-looking chairs that faced the command console. Also the bed that they had been laying on transformed into a huge pile of pillows on the floor of the command deck. There seemed to be passageways that led off of this main area, but none showed far enough to see where any of them went to. "It worked!" Ckaspian said, bursting out laughing. They all pulled off of each other and laid on the soft pillows.

Atomsk crawled over toward Ckaspian and made like he was going to go down on hir. "No, let me," Lilith said, stopping her husband. Instead, she leaned down and held the androgyne's penis up so that she could drink the sweet Elixir of Life from the lips of hir cunt. She drank of the moonflower deeply and tasted both of her lovers mixed together. Then, as if a natural reflex, Atomsk went down on Lilith, drinking Ckaspian's semen and the taste of his wife's sex on hir seed.

"Where we're going we don't need roads," Ckaspian said cryptically and cracked hirself up. "Come on, Buck, you can get in on this. Here, lay down right here." The strange hermaphroditic space being stood up and instructed Buck to lay down comfortably on the pillows. Then Ckaspian maneuvered hirself into reverse cowgirl position and guided his hard cock into hir ass. "Oh, Buck, uhhh, fuck," s/he moaned as s/he felt Buck's thick cock stretch hir asshole out. "Now you," Ckaspian motioned for Atomsk to come join in, his cock still rock-hard. In a moment he was on his knees in front of Ckaspian who was riding his brother's cock with hir ass. Atomsk guided his dick forward until he was sliding inside this strange creature's vagina. The cock attached to this vagina was fully erect and standing straight up, waiting for a pussy to ride it. Lilith came up and at it from the side, flipping her leg over like she was getting into a saddle. Then she sat down onto it, taking Ckaspian's cock into her again.

For a few moments they were all four of them joined sexually. Their genitals were locked and they began to gyrate and thrust. There was no rhyme or rhythm to it, just Chaos—but it was fun, ecstatic, euphoric, blissful even. Their sex became amorphous, Soulminds and bodies melting into each other to the point where none of them knew where they ended and the other began. No matter how fun it was, they couldn't hold that position for long and they found themselves fallen on the pillows again, floundering in each other's legs and sex fluids. They all began to laugh hysterically. "This is a strange little spaceship tryst," Lilith said smiling, her hands between her thighs. "I think it helped that we smoked a fat blunt before coming back here. Our magick did its work. Trippy as fuck though." She looked around at the inside of *The Quantum Shortbus*. Looking across the pillow pit of naked bodies at her husband, she said, "I feel like you have this whole other secret life with Calvin I didn't know about. Building rocket ships and transforming genders. I only got a lousy Tarot card reading."

"Hey, we had more than that," Ckaspian retorted, slapping Lilith playfully on the leg.

"We did have more than that, didn't we?" she replied. "But now that you have your spaceship, not-alien, are you leaving?"

"Well, that's what I wanted to ask you all," s/he continued. "Now that we're all lovers. I'm going to travel off-planet for a while and explore the Spiralverse and even beyond that. Will you come with me?"

Atomsk and Lilith exchanged a glance. "Be your companions in space?" she said, almost not believing her ears.

"Yeah, what do you have to lose?" Ckaspian said excitedly. "It could be fun!"

"I feel like my place is here," Buck answered. "I have the junkyard and my inventions and art that need attending to."

"But we could...go," Atomsk said slowly, looking at his wife.

"Yes, we want to be with you, Ckaspian," Lilith said, looking up out of the one window that was above the command console, she could see the side of the barn and the light of the morning shining in with golden rays through the slats. "Let's get some stuff and we'll be ready to leave. Fuck this place! I want to visit other galaxies!" She jumped up naked, throwing pillows with her tits bouncing. Magickally all their clothes were in neat piles by the white wall. They all got their clothes back on quickly and wondered how they were going to get back out to regular reality. The inside of the spaceship seemed to be pretty stable which was a testament to the strength of Ckaspian's spell—well, hir spell backed by all their juicy orgasms.

Waving hir hand toward the other three, energy bubbles the colors of their Soulminds appeared around them. Ckaspian's yellow bubble floated hir up off the floor and then through the wall. The energy of hir Soulmind guided the rest of them out after hir. When they were all standing on the floor of the barn again, their auras faded and disappeared. "We're gonna go pack a couple bags," Atomsk said as he took his wife's hand and led her out the door of the barn and back to their car.

"Get this thing out on the runway!" They heard Lilith yell right before the car door shut and they sped away.

"You heard the woman, you androgynous alien fruitcake," Buck said jokingly.

"I'm not an alien," Ckaspian laughed.

"No, but you want to be," Buck replied, giving hir a wink. He went over to the main barn doors and unlatched them.

When he pushed them they swung open easily. "Let's get your space cruiser out onto the 'runway.'" He paused. "Well, it's not really a runway, it's just a flat strip that runs through the middle of the junkyard. It's dusty, relatively flat with some gravel. I think you could build up some good speed."

"Will my cum be enough?" s/he asked dreamily, staring at the sky.

"Oh, your cum will most definitely be enough," Buck said confidently. "And you'll be flying with two people who drank the Elixir of Life. I think that more than guarantees you safe passage at least out of the Earth's atmosphere." After saying this he walked out into the junkyard so he could direct *The Quantum Shortbus* to the makeshift runway.

It was strange for Ckaspian to captain the spaceship from the new command console. The spacial distortion was something to get used to—feeling the inside to be so large but then looking out of the windshield and seeing what was really outside the van. Using the holographic keypad and joystick, Ckaspian steered the *Shortbus* around and drove it out of the barn and into the glory of the morning Sun. S/he drove it over to the beginning of a long strip between piles of junk and trashed cars next to where Buck was standing.

A half hour later Atomsk and Lilith showed back up with a few packed bags. Ckaspian was standing next to Buck outside of *The Quantum Shortbus* waiting for them. S/he opened hir hands and produced three yellow plasma balls floating above hir palms. Throwing them at the luggage, the energy orbs expanded to be like bubbles' and encapsulated the bags. Ckaspian pointed with hir thumb at the spaceship and then the yellow orbs floated the bags into the side of the van, disappearing into the spaceship within. "Are you ready?" Ckaspian asked.

"Ready as we'll ever be," Lilith said.

Atomsk nodded his agreement. "To the next stage of evolution."

"To the next stage of evolution," Ckaspian echoed back. "And to the evolution of the relationship. On a quantum level." S/he stepped forward and took hir companions' hands in hirs. All three of their auras illuminated and Ckaspian made them all levitate off of the ground and float into *The Quantum Shortbus*. After they were inside the spaceship, Lilith noticed that their luggage was placed nicely in the corner. She ran over to one of her bags and unzipped it. What she pulled out was a garment, a long robe.

"This is for you," she said, bringing the robe over to Ckaspian. "I made it—and yes, I do make clothes." As Lilith held up the garment, s/he marveled at its beauty and uniqueness. It was like something OSHO would wear. It was a long blue robe and the shoulder pads were spikes and came out over the shoulders. Ckaspian was soon out of hir clothes and wriggling hir way into this one. S/he loved it.

"Thank you so much," the space being said in gratitude. "It's sort of futuristic and yet androgynous. Totally my style as a cosmic slut."

Lilith laughed. "Should we get this thing moving?"

Atomsk had already walked over to the command console and was looking at the holographic keypad and joystick. "How do we take off?" he asked.

Suddenly they heard Buck's voice yelling from outside. "Don't forget to come back to Earth and visit me!"

Atomsk smiled. "We couldn't forget you, Buck," he yelled back. "We'll come back and see you soon."

Ckaspian had approached the console now and hit a couple keys on the holographic display, engaging the thrusters. The tires were also spinning, gaining speed as fire spat out the back. "Will we get up to speed in time?" Lilith asked.

"I don't doubt it," Ckaspian replied, pushing the joystick up to a higher speed. "If I can think it, it can happen."

Just as their speed reached its peak and the nose of The Quantum Shortbus began to lift up, Machandi suddenly appeared in their midst. Both Atomsk and Lilith gaped at the sight of this semi-translucent alien before them. "I knew there was something alien around here!" Lilith exclaimed. "Nothing of great importance in evolution ever comes about without extraterrestrial intervention. Our DNA has been tampered with by alien beings after all. To evolve into a Starseed is the next stage in our metamorphosis."

"You're the one I saw while doing Angelic work with Klarissa," Atomsk remarked.

Machandi walked over to Ckaspian at the control console. "You better pray to the Unified Field that you can get out of the atmosphere and break from Earth's gravity."

"Watch how easy this is," Ckaspian said with a wink and a cheeky grin. S/he pulled the joystick back and they began to go vertical, the thrusters rumbling behind them. Then they were off the ground, they had liftoff. Atomsk and Lilith just stood in the background staring mesmerized through the windshield which was now the viewport. They were up into the blue sky and then through the clouds. Then they were high enough to see a shimmering sea of stars on a black void.

Suddenly there was a rip in space-time right next to Ckaspian and s/he heard an ethereal voice call hir name. The portal opened and Ckaspian gazed through and saw hirself as if through the distortions of the waves on a pond. "You're going to need this temporary Christ-Consciousness net from my future in order to get through the Prison Grid around Earth," the future Ckaspian's voice said as s/he threw a ball of green plasma that looked like a light-net made of a flexible grid. This green net of energy wrapped completely around the present Ckaspian, went through hir heart and then expanded out and around the whole *Quantum Shortbus*. A strange looking blue grid appeared above them around the Earth like it was a barrier between them and space. When the green net around *The Quantum Shortbus* came near this blue grid, the blue grid decayed and crumbled, leaving a hole for them to fly right through.

Once they were through the Prison Grid, it healed itself behind them as they flew out into deep space. They were floating through the blackness toward the bright white of the Moon. Since they were through the barrier, the green Christ-Consciousness net around them faded and then disappeared.

"Oh, yeah, that was easy," Machandi laughed.

"Easy for an advanced god," Ckaspian said, feigning importance. "Now all planets can be dillywapped by my magickal cock and I'll be eaten out by nebulous dark nebulas."

"So you're ready to go fuck the cosmos?" Machandi said, gesturing out toward the stars.

"To fuck the cosmos and cum-spray stars into the void," Ckaspian said dramatically. "That is my mission. I've built galaxies with my orgasms and now I vibrate them with my love."

*"I demand from the universe the greatest degree of freedom of which I can conceive. I demand that the universe teach me about even greater degrees of freedom than I can currently conceive. I demand answers from the universe that will satisfy my capacity to understand anything that I wish to know. I demand the fullest degree of pleasure and happiness of which I am capable. I demand the freedom to demand. I demand the ability to play any game that I can conceive of an intelligence (still an anthropomorphic projection) playing at the 'level' of creating universes, interacting with other intelligences of the same or other kinds at that level in whatever modes of interaction I prefer or wish to create."*

- Neil Freer, *God Games*

The Rosicrucians called a man who attained all-consciousness, thus making the two poles conscious within him, a 'hermaphrodite' – composed of Hermes and Aphrodite – and depicted him with two heads. He is master of sexual energy, of the dragon, the 'lord of this world'; he stands on the dragon, who in turn rules the earth. The all-conscious man uses the dragon's fire to stimulate and keep active his higher nerve and brain centres.

**- Elisabeth Haich, "Sexual Energy and Yoga"**

Avtar Simrit is a mystery even unto hirself. Know Thyself, as Neo said in *The Matrix*. If you know yourself then you know me well. Avtar Simrit is neither here nor there; neither this nor that; neither high nor low. And if you want to fuck around and find out, she might just chop your ego up with a machete. :-) www.mc-pan.com